With an incredible eye for the nuances of New Orleans, America's most interesting city, Michael Allen Zell presents crime fiction with verve, grit, and tenderness. The characters in *The Last Shadow* are people I've known from a distance. Zell's talent allows readers to have access to the hidden dreams and terrors of their lives.

—Maurice Carlos Ruffin, author of *The American Daughters*

Zell demonstrates a gallows humor and a fine ear for entertainment…like the best crime fiction, the story invests deeply in setting, and it succeeds by virtue of its author's palpable love for New Orleans and the people who live there.

—*Los Angeles Review of Books*

What really keeps us turning pages is Zell's authorial voice, his insights into human nature, and the dark sense of humor that comes out of observing city life.

—*The New Orleans Advocate*

Rebel Soul

by Michael Allen Zell

Copyright © 2026 by Michael Allen Zell and MBW

All rights reserved. No part of this work may be reproduced or transmitted in any form or by any means (except by a reviewer who may quote brief passages for the purposes of review) without permission in writing from the publisher.

Printed in the U.S.A.

ISBN 979-8-9899197-3-4

This is a work of fiction. Names, characters, places, businesses, events, and incidents are either the product of the author's imagination or used in a fictitious manner. Any resemblance to actual persons, living or dead, or actual events is purely coincidental.

REBEL SOUL

ABOUT THE AUTHOR

Michael Allen Zell is a New Orleans-based novelist, journalist, screenwriter, and playwright.

Michaelallenzell.com
Instagram.com/michaelallenzell

To Jessica

REBEL SOUL

Michael Allen Zell

Even a kid barely brought up in a shabby home on a bloody block in the sinking city knew the same thing the suits and the boots knew. The third act is where you get your lick back. It just got called different names by different people but had been happening in the same city in different decades with the same mindset and carried out differently.

The kids weren't dumb. Far from it. Just kept intentionally uneducated. Been that way. They saw it. You have to get yours. Learned it. Knew their turn was coming to live it. Whatever happens after that, so be it. Just how it was. Couldn't face anyone if you didn't. The real New Orleans code. Messy. Tradition. Been that way. Realize the realization, retreat from your defeat, prepare for the comeback, and hit strong when they don't expect it. Been that way.

1 When The Wind Blows

Maya disappeared. Went off the grid, Maya did, throwing away her digital footprint once the hefty insurance payout ended up in the mailbox which rose like a white flag of defeat in front of the neglected yard that no longer held a house. No more Aunt Nekisha either, whose soul had left the block and was now amidst a different grid of space and time. As far as the neighbors were concerned, they thought the same had happened to Maya. Elijah, her stepbrother, too. Consequences from getting on the wrong side of the Mafia.

"It's time."

How does one simply go off the grid without a trace in a digital world? Easy if willing to give up a phone, computer, bank account, car, social media, and anything else traceable, trackable, and potentially attackable. Even communication with Attorney Jason Polidore, who Maya had working on her parents' court case, was handled by a regular in-person monthly meeting way off the street grid most were familiar with.

Again, "It's time."

These meetings happened for many moons, because Maya was recharging and regrouping. As the clock ticked across the 35 meetings that had passed, Vinh Nguyen, the Rizzo crime family, and Flora Mosley were convinced and complacent that Maya had fled far away from the urban swampland of New Orleans and the nicest and meanest people you could ever meet.

In fact, she'd been there all along. In the woods. Off the grid. Made a tough pilgrimage. Traded her digital footprint for dirt. Trees too. Down by where the Mississippi River makes a curlicue to punctuate its way to the Gulf of Mexico.

"It's time," she said to Polidore at their 36th meeting in late 2027. Not far from where she was staying but still a bridge away.

How are the precise number of meetings known, those that took place atop the levee near dumped trash, modest homes, and former horse stables at the end of the long road in an area called the Cut Off? Known as such, not because it's actually cut off from the rest of civilization. It's part of the New Orleans street grid after all, but, truth be told, it feels like it is cut off. Geographically and for familiarity. The number of meetings Maya and Polidore had are not known due to omniscience. Not due to speculation either.

The answer is far simpler. She is me. I'm Maya Liara Gaines who disappeared for the past 1,100 days. She is me and it's time.

Elijah closed the notebook he'd been fervently writing in and placed the pen on top of it.

"Sounds good," he said. "But one thing."

Maya responded, "What's that?"

"Why you doing this?" he asked, gesturing at the notebook by habit, not for Maya's sake. "If it gets found, it's evidence. You dry snitchin'."

"Elijah. The outcome is the outcome. The way is the way. I can't be concerned about the result. Plus, if someone comes here and finds the notebook, that means they already know."

He paused.

"I'm worried that…"

"You mean all we've been preparing for."

Maya knew well everything unspoken behind his three words. That Elijah's mother Mimi was a mess and her boyfriend Pigeon had kicked him out of the house. That Promise Home, the last resort homeless shelter for children where Elijah had gone, was a façade to pimp out the kids for dates or parties that the Rizzo's hosted for politicians, pro athletes, and more. That Elijah had narrowly escaped from the same house fire that took the physical life of Aunt Nekisha. That, though Maya was still disappointed with her father over having a child outside his marriage, it didn't matter at this point. She and Elijah were the only family the other had. Polidore had informed her at their 4th meeting that Franklin and Eugenia, Maya's parents, had been killed inside their respective Federal pens. She knew who was behind it. Even more was at stake now.

"Don't worry. It'll be alright," she assured.

"There you go."

"Unh unh. Too early for me to give you a sass pass. Let's join the group."

They both rose from their chairs. Surrounding them was a bookcase, three two-level bunk beds, several cushions on the outskirts of the floor, and a small desk that Elijah now stood over. Other than the cushions, everything else was made with wood by hand. The small house itself too. Tucked in the woods in an area far less habitated and geographically familiar than even the Cut Off.

They walked through a living room adjacent to the

kitchen, more so a kitchenette, since much of the cooking was done outside over a flame. Maya didn't need Elijah to assist her in walking to the front door. She knew the steps well and could easily sense him behind her as a sign of respect.

The door opened to a scene with two rows of three people doing a martial arts warm-up very similar to what Maya had learned in the City Park classes under old oaks with Sifu Julius Mosley. Though he had passed on, his influence lived in the hearts and minds of countless others beyond Maya. His daughter Flora was another story.

"One, two, three, four," rang out from Ayana leading the others, who also counted aloud, guiding Maya not only to the correct place in the exercise but also to which spot was open for her. Ayana was a Xavier University graduate from two years past. Her jobs as a biomedical scientist and bartender, as well as her sweet nature and anti-establishment mindset, served well for Maya's plans.

Of the others, Nevaeh, Felipe, and Cookie had their days at Promise Home with Elijah, and each had a unique skill. Zachary, who was the sole white member and the oldest of the group with seven years beyond Maya's 27-years-old, was a writer and martial artist she met at the Thai Buddhist temple in the adjacent part of the woods. Not a bad cook either.

The remaining member of the group was Tâm who was made an orphan when the crime boss Nguyen, who ran the Vietnamese area called Versailles, had her parents killed in a show of force five years before he'd seen Maya use her martial arts skills to handle a double robbery at the Elysian Fields gas station and push for her to work as his enforcer.

Young Tâm had been living in an abandoned 2nd floor business at the strip mall on Alcee Fortier, steps from Chef Menteur, where Nguyen's office and jewelry store were housed. Saw Maya come both times. First to tell Nguyen she'd take the job, and second in the commotion when she returned the money and put Nguyen on the ground along with his bodyguard Jimmy. The then-9-year-old had snuck into the back seat of Danh Trang's car when he drove Maya away from Versailles, jumped out of it when he dropped off Maya, and then lived in a series of abandoned houses close enough to study Maya. First by Aunt Nekisha's place near Mandeville and Derbigny. Next down the block from the 7th ward home that was firebombed. Finding empty houses in New Orleans was easy. Selling bottles of water to make money wasn't, but she got by.

Tâm had seen the fire and was biding her time until she followed Maya and Elijah when she spied them leaving with a suitcase weeks later. That made her the first of the six beyond Maya and Elijah, still the youngest member of the group, and exceptionally loyal to her benefactor. They called her Lil Bit, because she was. She was also a strong gardener.

Initially the founding three slept on the floor with beds that rolled up in the morning. As the group expanded, bunk beds were built to utilize space in the 725 square foot house. Maya and Lil Bit kept to Japanese style sleeping. First the tatami mat was spread across the floor. Upon it was placed a thin mattress called a shikibuton.

Once she rose in the morning, Maya tended to the

elaborate garden after rolling up her bed. She could tell by running her hand gently and steadily across the spinach leaves, the tomato cages, sweet potato vines, and all else if deer, raccoon, stray dog, coyote, or even a wild boar had helped themselves to a late-night dinner.

When she thought of the early days in the woods, that naïve period before realizing that animals harvesting from the garden meant humans might not have food for days, Maya recalled that she walked then as if the next step wasn't promised. Like it was a delicate dawn. Her mind was exaggerating the abundance of caution she moved with at that earlier time, but it was also true that she now flowed through the house and the trees as if she was born there.

Maya wasn't stumbling and fumbling around with her blindness. To the contrary, her other senses became heightened by necessity. This had stunned each new member at first until they eventually took for granted that Maya did things in a Maya kind of way. She demanded no special treatment from them. What she did demand was everything else.

2 The Heat's On

Step one happened on a Monday. Maya wanted to set the tone for the week. A bitter battlefield. Most people dread Mondays anyway. She had the group prepared, and each did their work late Sunday night.

They were modern ninjas. Night warriors. Get in by blending in, complete the task, and escape discreetly. The whole point of step one was to throw everyone on the list off-kilter from their normal baseline of life while having them think it was merely random bad luck.

"Noooo!" yelled Flora Mosley, slamming her hands against the steering wheel.

"What?"

"Do you not see the lights and hear the damn beeping, Brit? Saying I have two flat tires."

"Ohh. That's bad timing."

"Yeah. This is insane."

The two grumbled out of the car and Brit went over to where Flora was bent down and shaking her head at a long nail slightly protruding from the driver's side front tire. They repeated their moaning and groaning at the back tire.

"We're due in Houston at 3:00 for the pickup. The Rizzo's not gonna be happy."

"It's not your fault," said Brit.

"You think they fucking care? Party favors came in today. Can't leave 'em on the boat. Now they got to sit on it longer 'til we get there."

Brittany Casimir was the daughter of a City Councilman, roommate of her best friend Flora in a Warehouse District condo, and, if necessary, both were willing to use their looks and more to get out of a stop in Calcasieu Parish by the anti-drug task force.

She sighed while Flora held up her phone to make the dreaded call.

No longer than ten hours earlier, Nevaeh had entered the parking garage dressed all in black. Hood up to help conceal the knife scar across her left cheek. The one her own father had given her when she wouldn't sleep with him at age 13. The same thing he often did when drunk and her mom was at work.

"You little bitch! Now nobody gonna fuck you!" he'd mocked. Young Nevaeh bided her time. Sold bottles of water for $1.00 until she made enough to buy herself a knife with a 3-inch blade. Went to the Goodwill store and practiced slicing and dicing with couches, stuffed animals, dressers, and anything else she could until they finally caught on and kicked her out for good.

Her mom didn't want to deal with a kid, so Nevaeh ended up in Promise Home. That's where she met Elijah who made her laugh from the first time a few of them began to kiki. Same Elijah whose bunk bed was next to hers now. Same Elijah who gave her the assignment to slash the two tires and shove a nail into each hole so that it looked random.

When she heard about why this particular person's car was the target, it made the task feel good. This good wasn't as good, though, as the great good the first time she'd used the knife. Waited until her father left his drinking spot, Lucky's Lounge. He hadn't stumbled far along on Laine, toward their apartment on Grant two blocks down, before she snuck him from behind. Had been waiting in the shadows of the body shop across the street. Lacerated his larynx. Quick and deep. Had his chin bobbing so wildly she'd mocked, "Now who's the chicken head?" Choked on his own blood and died on the sidewalk a stone's throw from Chef Menteur.

By comparison, Joseph "Joey" Lyons had it well. His attorney, Nick Noto, had gotten the sordid video evidence from his parties all thrown out in court. Everything Maya had provided to Jason Polidore, who'd discreetly forwarded it to media, meant nothing. Charges got pinned and stuck like a demerit badge on Buchi, who only organized the fights in the warehouse under the Danziger Bridge, and he kept his mouth shut for a price.

"Dar! What the Sam hill is going on?" Joey bellowed.

A few seconds later, his wife Darlene padded along the second-floor hallway to look down upon Joey lying on his back across the marble downstairs floor.

"You fall down the stairs?"

"Stop! Stop!"

Joey's exhortations weren't enough to dissuade her from rushing down the staircase. She soon joined him in a heap on the floor after making sounds like ancient shouting.

"What the damn hellementary?" she groaned.

"Dar, you know I hate when you do that."

"Pick your priorities, my dear. Just look at us."

She reached down to touch the floor. "Why would they wax the floor late at night and not tell us?"

Joey looked at her oddly. "Smell it," he demanded.

She actively sniffed. "Smells like grease. Cooking grease."

"Yeah. It's pervasive. This was sloppiness. Somebody's getting fired today."

"They're not gonna be here for another hour."

"The hell they're not. I'm calling right now. Heads are gonna roll," boomed Joey.

Y'know, it kinda smells like McDonald's fries," Dar said.

The couple was in an even more foul mood after they slipped and took three more dives to the floor on the way to the kitchen. Joey Lyons may have been the boss of the top in-state construction firm, but he was feeling mighty powerless at the moment.

This was the work of Felipe, who had also met Elijah at Promise Home. As a young kid in Panama City, he was such a fast runner that everyone said he'd end up in the Olympics. That talk became a thing of the past once one of his older brothers forced him to help out with breaking and entering into Lakeview homes.

Now he had a skill but no gold medal on the horizon. It was easy enough work to disable the Lyons' security system, slip into the North Shore mansion late night, and drip used cooking grease from the McDonald's on De Gaulle at select spots across the floor. Old habits made him want to shove one of the smaller sculptures into his backpack, but he kept to Maya's instructions.

Shortly after the Lyons' slipped and slid, flopped and flipped, six phone calls rang with urgency almost simultaneously to two houses. "There are rats everywhere!" was proclaimed to Mafia boss Anthony Rizzo, his son Thomas, underboss Louis Rizzo, and his eldest, Louis Jr.

One was from Cefalu, the old school Italian joint in Mid-City, known to be Rizzo-owned. Three were from Bourbon Street tourist traps with a thin layer of ownership pointing away from the Rizzo's. The other two were Black-owned, at least on paper, because in reality the entrepreneur was merely the front man in the usual New Orleans tradition.

"Tommy, what the fuck is going on?" Anthony Rizzo spat at his son while both were getting an earful simultaneously.

"I DON'T KNOW!"

The elder Rizzo, who'd run the terrible empire for the past 43 years, raised his right index finger.

"You watch your fucking tone. Hear me?"

The chastened Thomas nodded in respect. "I dunno what's going on," he said. "It's New Orleans. All these restaurants got rats."

"Nah, this ain't regular."

"It was a full moon last night," tried Thomas.

"Excuse me," Anthony said to the phone. "I think my son just said rats are acting up due to the full moon. Lemme call you back in a minute."

Of course, in proper New Orleans fashion he didn't. Nor was it expected.

The father and son scene played out only with slight difference in Metairie.

"What's the big deal? Tourists gonna come back anyway. The Black joints, long as they think it's trendy, they be back waitin' in line an hour and takin' pics under the sign. We don't eat there anyway."

"Ohh yeah?" shot Louis Sr. He pointed at the phone. "This is Sal from Cefalu. Full of rats. At our place. He said it's three of 'em on the table in back."

"Cefalu?" groaned Louis Jr.

"We gotta get exterminators out there. I'll call Anthony. Nobody's gotta know."

"Too late," said the younger Rizzo while he held up his phone. A Bourbon St. tourist had shot video from the sidewalk. The open view through large windows showed a veritable rat party on the tables, chairs, and floor of Swampdog. The place had no redeeming value before, since salty bar food and watered-down drinks were the m.o., but it was about to be known internationally for another reason.

Elijah and Zachary had been busy before dawn. They hit the three neighborhood spots first since those closed earlier, then it was on to the French Quarter. Raw meat was retrieved from walk-in coolers, plopped onto the floor, tossed on tables, and slung over chairs.

They had barely left each restaurant before word got out by way of joyous rodent ultrasonic chatter that it was time to feast. By the time the managers and staff showed up to prep for lunch, the meat was all devoured, but the ravenous rats remained, seeking to continue their banquet.

Hours after the Rizzo's fielded multiple frantic calls, a hungover T-Boy moaned and rubbed his eyes. His half of the shotgun house he rented had threadbare sheets nailed above windows instead of curtains, and the noon sun was glaring.

"Uhhhh, dang," he muttered anmafd simultaneously scratched his head and crotch. Sat up in bed and stretched out his arms to full length.

"Shit."

Rubbed his eyes and walked to the kitchen. After some vape puffing, he picked up the half-full can of Miller High Life.

Spat it out immediately.

"Kuhhhplgh!"

T-Boy went next to his trusty bottle of Hennessy. No glass needed. Took a swig and couldn't get the liquid out of his mouth quickly enough.

"What the…"

This forced his hand to do something he'd never once attempted in his life. That's what it had come to. He grabbed the closest go cup he could find and stomped over to the sink. Pushed the lever back. T-Boy was going to drink water.

Third time was so vile it had him throwing the plastic cup as he spat out the water. Went back to the bedroom and continued to the bathroom sink, where he stuck his tongue out.

"Hmm." Looked the same as usual. A border of pink overpowered by sickly white, as if it were salmon left in the fridge for months.

No way he was going to the doctor. No chance he was going to sit there surrounded by unread magazines until an earnest young assistant called out, "Kantrell Teed." Not just because there was a 3-years-old open warrant on him from the whole mess with that chick fighter.

T-Boy didn't go to doctors. He sipped Henny instead

until his body got right. But now he couldn't even do that.

"Why's everything taste so bad?" he asked aloud, poking his tongue out again.

Ayana was especially suited for this role. With her background as both biomedical scientist and bartender, she'd concocted a clear liquid that was benign but so bitter as to be undrinkable. She'd had a special challenge, though, when he came home earlier than expected.

Ayana had only gotten to the sink faucet filter when she heard keys at the front door of the small apartment in the 9th ward 'cross the canal. She quickly grabbed the dropper and bottle of foul liquid to hide in the closet until he began loudly snoring 38 minutes later. She heard sounds in the meantime she wished to forget.

At that point, Ayana knew she should scurry out but was compelled to finish the job before leaving the corner of Deslonde and Derbigny.

Cookie and Lil Bit had a wholly different type of task way out in New Orleans East, but they'd been able to start much earlier than all the others.

They'd gone to the back of *Tốt Nhất* Jewelry Store with a long garden hose. From there it was a simple matter for Cookie to use her gymnastics ability and scale the building up to the second floor. Over 20 years ago, there had been an apartment for rent, but now no one was disturbed when she jimmied the window loose and entered.

"Turn it on?" Lil Bit called out in a loud but muffled voice.

"Not yet," from the window.

Cookie had the end of the hose tied around her waist

like an odd belt. Better that than Lil Bit try to throw the hose all the way up to the second floor.

Cookie checked to make sure there were no obvious holes in the floor and that the front windows were solidly secured. The next step was a little tricky, only because she didn't want to go out the front door and risk being seen or on camera.

First, she crawled back out through the window, pulling it down behind her to within a few inches from its resting base. As Cookie hung on for dear life, she then untied the hose with one hand and threw at least three feet of it sideways into the room.

"Now," Cookie called out to Lil Bit, who dutifully turned the faucet all the way on. The hose kicked to life soon enough and began to pulse like an awakened snake swallowing in reverse.

Once water began to pour into the 2nd floor space, Cookie pulled the window down a little more to hold the hose in place before she made her way back to the ground. At that point they waited.

Maya had calculated an expected flow rate of 15 GPM (Gallons Per Minute) would make for just under 2 1/3 cubic feet of water every minute. Elijah had found on the Orleans Parish assessor's website that the second floor was 1,000 square feet. That meant it would take 1,000 cubic feet to fill the 2nd floor with one foot of water. Maya divided 1,000 by 2 1/3 to find it would take about 430 minutes or seven hours, for a full one foot of water to build up and sit on the decaying floor.

Shortly before 2AM, Cookie and Lil Bit had turned off the water, pulled the hose loose, and raced off. By

4:00AM, weight of water had caused the groaning 2nd floor to collapse, making a soggy mess of the jewelry store below and setting off piercing alarms.

Manager Tien Ly knew she would get an earful from her boss, so she tried to first prepare him before relaying the word of bad news.

"Get to the fuckity fuck point," he hissed over a fuzzy connection. Since his FCI Terre Haute jailbreak, he'd been hiding out in an area not near many people or a phone tower.

Vinh Nguyen got even angrier when he heard what had happened, especially since the building didn't even have a sprinkler system. As expected, though, Maya Gaines' name was the furthest thing from his mind.

3 The Path Walked Alone

There's a Japanese word, Johatsu, which means to vanish into thin air and start over in another place. What else can you do when you wake up blind the morning after your aunt was killed for your actions after you were blackmailed when you took the first move in reconciling with your father?

You go away from others. Your proximity to them only brings death to those you love. You had been so focused on wondering if what was in you would elevate or sink you that you failed to consider how what was in you might impact others.

You isolate. No one else can get hurt that way. You devote your feverish life to becoming an intense warrior.

You think, "Where's the furthest place to be away from people?" Your mind goes to two places. One, way out past Versailles, the Vietnamese area in New Orleans East, hits too hard. History there. The wrong kind. Plus, alligators in the swamps.

The second place rises to the top immediately. You recall Sifu Julius Mosley renting a van to take your martial arts class to a place you didn't know existed.

First, you crossed the river before heading through the West Bank until crossing a second bridge. You eventually saw a long fence surrounding nice homes until Sifu announced, "English Turn. Not our destination," before he turned left into the woods.

Sifu who believed in you when no one did, including

yourself. Sifu who you knew was truly honored to be your mentor and who you also sensed wished you were his daughter. And Sifu who you sadly visited on his death bed, seeing a once strong, assured, wise man reduced to a shell of himself.

This Sifu drove into the woods. You thought it was a little scary. Others in the van felt the same way, except you all knew Sifu would protect you.

He stopped a short time after, near a unique building. Sifu pronounced two words you'd not heard before then and followed them with "Buddhist temple. Keep your mind open."

You're glad you had your sight then so you could experience walking up the sixteen steps, before pausing to take off your shoes, and proceeding into the temple.

You had never seen anything like it before. So ornate yet functional. There must have been nine monks seated in front. They made a long row and all held a piece of string that ran from end to end.

After the ceremony and your first encounter with delicious Thai food, Sifu asked a question while the group headed back to the van. For someone on a higher level, he asked a lot of questions. You've never forgotten that.

"Why were the monks holding the string?"

You weren't a pick-me, so you waited for the others, but no one answered.

"To show how interconnected we all are?" you asked rather than stated.

"Keep going."

"If one of the monks moved, it impacted all the others," you added more firmly.

Sifu nodded. "Right now, they're cutting the string to make bracelets for each of them. They would've probably offered them to us as well. As a blessing for good luck. Protection. I wanted to make sure the regulars got theirs, though. When a room or group is not of your own, you get in where you fit in. Move quietly. Take time to understand."

You noticed he subtly focused on the others in the group, who were white. You were Black like Sifu, so this was a given in existing safely or trying to avoid those who would act too familiar.

After that, you visited the temple at least once more before you went to the eye doctor to find a rare genetic disease had taken your sight at a young age. You held it together as best you could, not only for Elijah's sake, but also your own. Falling into a deep depression wasn't an option.

Instead, you worked on your O&M, orientation and mobility, with Elijah so you would feel comfortable using a cane. At least initially. You made sure Jason Polidore had the evidence from the mansion about what Promise Home and the others were up to.

Once that was complete, you took some of the money from one of the canning jars that had been buried in the yard, and you traveled down to the woods. You realized quickly how much trust you had to have in others to take you the 13-mile stretch to the far recesses of New Orleans. For an independent person, that was not a lesson you liked learning, but you had no choice.

The woods offered a place to sit, to grieve, to flail your arms, to mourn, to scream, to hurt, to hit trees, and to be still for eight days and eight nights.

You had been dropped off at the Buddhist temple, so you followed the nearby tree line until getting far enough away from the unpaved road until you turned into the woods and found a spot to settle.

If mosquitoes dive-bombed you, so be it. If snakes bit you, so be it. If ants made your skin feel under siege, so be it. This was where you, Maya Gaines, would remake yourself. You were built for it.

It had been a couple days full of mourning and exercising, stillness and action, before you had your first visitor. He didn't speak English. You didn't speak Thai. But you realized soon enough that he was clearly a monk from the temple.

When he said, "Kin, kin," you thought he must be tremendously wrongheaded, but he kindly put the berries in your hand and gently placed his palm under your hand to push it toward your mouth. That's when you understood that he was saying, "Eat, eat."

You connected the dots in your mind. Though you didn't know what he looked like, you could hear genuine sincerity and understood that he was merely out picking blackberries. You had simply decided to settle in the spot right where he harvested.

It was no stretch when, fully natural, he said, "*Ma kab chan*," which you learned means, "Come with me," as he took your hand in his so he could guide you out of the woods.

When you headed toward the Wat Wimuttayaram Buddhist Temple, you still used your bo staff to make sure you weren't about to walk into a tree, but it felt refreshing.

He knew you could handle it yourself, but he saw himself as serving you. Why deny a person that?

The hours you sat with the monks. Meditating, eating Som Tam—the Thai Papaya Salad, and listening while they chanted. All of it made you think of "we." You wondered if they thought the same thing, but that wasn't the kind of thing you ask, even if one of the monks had pretty good English, while you knew absolutely no Thai.

What he did say once you thanked them all and announced that you were going to return to the woods, was, "Would you like Kamon to accompany you back to your place?"

You learned from that. Kamon was the name of the berry picker. You also picked up upon the word "accompany" instead of "help" or "guide" and you wondered if he chose that word for kindness or it was merely random. You also felt like they saw you as "we."

You definitely felt it further when one of them spoke, and Anan translated, "We hope you return. Please don't let my gassiness keep you from it. Well, his," while the others laughed or chided.

Truth be told, you had smelled the fart earlier. The kind your father, rest in peace, had called silent but deadly, because you receive no trumpet-like warning before the pungent aroma fills your nostrils.

"I will be back. The smell of trash will not stop me, but you might need a new robe," went over very well when Anan translated it into Thai for the rest of them.

They responded in a completely different way, when you said, "I am grateful to Kamon for discovering me and introducing me to your group, but I'll return to the woods by myself."

You could hear each respond in some type of stunned fashion. You suspect at least one of them doubted at that point you were truly blind. You also suspect that at least one monk thought that the blind must have superpowers. The reason you suspected both of these things is because that has been your experience ever since with most others.

Counting steps, detecting changes around you, actively engaging in your other senses, and all the other things that were only beginning to develop back then also make people feel less guilty, so more comfortable. After all, it's often hard enough for many to make conversation once they learn you're blind, since that's apparently similar to being from another planet. If they can observe you doing your thing, then they don't feel guilty or obligated, though they'll remain suspicious of you.

You grew fond of the monks over the following few days. They made an ointment for you similar to Dit Da Jow after they saw you had calluses from using the bo staff and had been striking trees to condition your palms, fingertips, knuckles, and forearms. You suspect they also knew you were heavily meditating, doing handstands against trees, and spending so long in deep horse stance that it brought tears to your eyes.

They changed your life for the better. It reminded you of what Sifu Mosley had admitted a few years back, that when stumbling through Columbus Park in Chinatown, New York, looking for trouble, "I came upon two men sitting on a bench. One younger. One older. The younger one, who eventually became my Sifu—Tak Wah Eng is his name—said, 'The way you are living, the good spirit in you cannot grow.' The older man, who I learned was Grandmaster Wai Hong nodded. Shortly after this I poured my alcohol down the drain and found *The Last Shadow* book on the street. Sifu is the one who taught me Fu Jow Pai. Tiger Claw."

Anan assisted you with contacting Aunt Nekisha's friends and colleagues you'd heard her mention. From her dear friend Trishelle Odoms to your stepbrother Elijah, everyone was notified the day before the funeral.

That way it was less likely for all of those running and gunning for you to hear about it and get their shot. A far better chance for you to attend the funeral in disguise, settle matters, and return to the woods.

Funny thing—funny as in the unpredictability of laughing—not funny as humorous, was that you firmly expected to return to the woods after the funeral and continue to live for at least a little while as you did for eight days and eight nights.

When Elijah read the mail that named you as beneficiary of Aunt Nekisha's life insurance policy, when he said, "You have to make a claim, but it's for $500,000. Says you get the money in 60 days or less," when it struck you that the people behind the firebombing must've paid off NOFD, NOPD, and the insurance company, but that it ironically ended up benefiting you, it hit you so hard you could barely stand up.

You recall breathing rapidly and putting your hands on your thighs. The enormity of it all hit you. That Johatsu, to vanish into thin air, was firmly within reach. That the farting of one gassy monk would not keep you away, and, in fact, you were going to take them up on their offer to stay with them, bringing along Elijah and Lil Bit, until the insurance payout came. "Kin, kin" or "Come, come" took on double meaning.

You felt you were making Sifu proud, Sifu who initially brought you to the temple. Sifu who would likely have done as you did and chosen to live in the woods to grieve, rebuild, and think. Numb and methodical from missing stability eventually became a dominant warmth from new radiating life and labor.

You were learning the necessity to trust others in many ways at that time. Stunned too with the grace others extended to you. The Thai monks who sold you the adjacent plot of land with the woods and berries so you could build a house there, removing only as many trees as absolutely necessary. Your attorney, Jason Polidore, who agreed with your idea that he buy the lot to keep you off the grid finance-wise with the contractor who would let you, Elijah, and Lil Bit assist with the build. Keeping it all in Polidore's name meant that "Maya Gaines" wasn't on chain of title, not seen in public record, and allowed no easy way for Vinh Nguyen, the Rizzo's, Flora Mosley, or anyone else to find you.

These were the same public records, of course, that helped Zachary and Elijah in discovering things like the various restaurants owned by the Rizzo's, the home addresses of those on your list, and barely scratched the surface in how deeply connections ran in New Orleans.

It didn't take long for you to learn something that caused a shift in thinking. You, like many born or raised in New Orleans, who would meet others with a question about which high school they attended, didn't realize. The transplants didn't realize either.

Your shift in thinking was this: Before researching, you considered that New Orleans was a city with great culture where things didn't often work right. The Mafia was a thing of the past. Instead, you came to learn it's a Mafia city. Organized crime being tight with politicians and business people was in large part why things didn't often work right. The great culture was in spite of this. The hustle was because of this.

You appreciated the hustle of the people. Understood it. The nurse who sold hot plates. The college student who mowed loans. The delivery driver who started a remote bartending service. The aesthetician who sold sno-balls at second line parades. People tried to make due, but others thrived while standing on their backs. It wasn't right.

"Maya, you'd have to be crazy like a daisy to think anything will change," you said to yourself. Regardless, you still needed to do what you needed to do. Payback is payback.

4 Keep Your Head To The Sky

"You ever known me not to be?"

"Think you can beat him?"

"Hell, no. It's rigged, but Leon Mancuso has been unopposed every election for 38 years. Why? Because he's a Mafia judge. The biggest one in the city. I want to do two things. Shed some light on his shady ass and make him sweat."

"Didn't an election happen last month?"

"Yes, but I'm gonna push publicly for him to be removed from office for corruption and malfeasance. He gets removed, then there would be a special election."

"Where's this coming from?"

"Maya, you know what? Maybe I'm inspired by you. Plus, his drunk driving incident last month is a good catalyst to bring up other things."

Maya laughed at his victory talk. "I can't figure out if you're brave or crazy."

He responded in kind with his own hearty version. "Both. A brave crazy-ass attorney who's sick and tired of being sick and tired. And look who's talking."

Polidore looked around at the power lines atop the levee further down, the trees blocking his view of the Mississippi River, and the small houses across the street.

"I get it," she said before he could speak. "It's time."

"Why'd you want to meet up here in the first place? I could've come to your house. Why this spot? All these months."

She didn't need to think before answering. Gave him a benign glance.

"I like the breeze. The sound of the crickets. Boats humming on the river. Hearing the leaves rustle tells me no one on the Chalmette side of the river can see us. Trees in the way. Here in the Cut Off feels like the end of the world. Almost."

"Y'all really down here," he said. "Need anything?"

"We're all good. Thanks, though. You heard me? It's time."

He paused. "I heard you."

"That why you changed the subject?"

"Look, Maya. I fully understand why you want to do this."

"But. You're about to say, 'But X, Y, and Z.' Jason, this is what I've spent the past three years preparing for. Focused on it."

"I know," he said.

"I'm doing what I need to do. This isn't wild and random. My list has six people on it. No more, no less. Don't worry about me. There are three steps to this. The first one will be underway by this time tomorrow. It's time."

"Alright," Polidore said, but he didn't mean it. He was devoted to her cause, always appreciated true talk, but he feared he would end up only as a faithful witness to Maya's memory.

Not 24 hours later, Felipe sat in the woods meditating in the way Maya had shown him. Not fully clearing his mind but a very different style.

He consciously thought of the group, family, friends, people he liked, those he hated who had brought him nothing but the numb cuts of life, even those on Maya's list, and he took in their pain. Absorb it into himself before sending out positive blessings to them.

Done right it could be exhausting. These weren't nameless faceless people. Felipe still held a grudge against Luis for taking him down a bad road. His older brother Eduardo might have pushed him to be an eventual track star if not always traveling for work. But Luis did no more than ordered, "Come on," to an eighth grader, drove up Canal Blvd. and picked whether left or right to turn for a house to thieve.

The first time, left was the choice, which was suitable, since Felipe's life gradually went left too. They never got caught by NOPD. Didn't once have a homeowner fire a shot at them. None of that.

It didn't matter. Breaking, entering, and thieving took Felipe away from what he loved, what was now no more than a vacant desire. To add insult to injury, he was good at picking locks. Better than Luis too. That was a skill he never expected to master in middle school.

Speaking of, he wasn't long for school. Luis had him skipping classes since daytime was the best time to hit houses, while evenings were optimal for cars. They never knew what they'd find inside the Lakeview homes, but most had something good to take. Cars were different. A few people were lax enough to leave money or electronics in the vehicle, but Luis was searching for guns in the glove box or middle console.

The way it all became Felipe's great undoing started

at the house on Colbert St. He was in awe of the metal fence, a walkway leading through a grass lawn, and a porch with six pillars and two chairs.

"Don't even have to sit on the stoop," he said to the Luis who replied, "Shut up, stupid."

The facade was plain, white paint and brick, but the interior featured sculptures and paintings. It didn't matter that most were too large to thieve. What would they do with all that anyway?

An X-box or an air fryer was an easy sale, but the people Luis dealt with were out of their element with museum-quality pieces. Still, the two took what they could. The fancy egg Felipe grabbed was his great undoing.

Luis always gave him something small for his payment, but this time Felipe insisted on the red egg with gold on it. The metal sphere opened up to store jewelry inside, and Felipe knew Valentina, who he had a crush on, would be feeling him after she received the gift.

She didn't have a chance to see it, because Felipe's mother discovered the little treasure hidden in his sock drawer. She knew immediately. Her already-existing suspicions were born out by the object that resembled a $1,000,000 Faberge egg, though it retailed at around $75.

"You want to be in the streets? Go live there! You take after the Chong side, not the Castillo's!"

Luis and Felipe were immediately kicked out of the apartment on 4th St. on the half-empty block between South Dorgenois and South Rocheblave.

Luis had friends to crash with across the river in Marrero, so Felipe was on his own. Promise Home was it for him, where he quickly befriended Elijah over their love for corny jokes. He was the first of three from Promise Home who Elijah convinced Maya to take in the group way out in the woods.

Speaking of Promise Home, City Hall and local media wanted nothing to do with the fallout of a story about distinguished citizens being involved with prostitutes and kids from the last resort children's shelter. Staff member Monica Delatte, who was actively involved in the sordid arrangements, had fled the state, so that was all the better as far as the city was concerned.

It meant, as a sort of silver lining, that Promise Home wasn't closed, so the 200 or so kids staying there had a place for as long as they needed it. The number included Cookie and Nevaeh.

Cookie grew up feeling her life was unique. She spent the longest time at the house on Old Roman St. in part of a tangled group of streets that confounded in its layout.

"Do that trick again," neighbors would say, and she would perform a child's approximation of the gymnastic floor routine that had so transfixed her during the 2021 Olympics.

"For a cookie," she'd say, and soon enough no one ever called her "Zenobia" again. Not "Zen," "Nobi," or "Bia" either. Not only because she had a sweet tooth. Cookie, like over 20,000 Black children in New Orleans, didn't know when the next meal was coming. Were there funds allocated for this? Yes. Were those funds redirected or outright stolen? Also, yes.

Had Cookie known this, her scraped spirit would've turned into acute anger to fill her soul, but since she was fully aware that there was always someone to impress for food, the child turned into a priestess of optimism. Many of those who lived by Cookie in the 7th ward had little more than her own mother did for cooking and to provide for her three siblings.

What to do?

"I'm going to the Quarters," Cookie announced for the first time to her mother at age twelve, but she didn't bother after that. Tourists were easy cash. She kept her distance from the other kids playing drums on buckets for their own meals.

Plus, she had a different unique skill.

"Hey Mister. Wanna see me climb that building?" She'd point to a Bourbon Street spot. "I bet you $5 I can go up to the second floor."

She'd typically shimmy up the balcony support posts, scale the cast iron, hop up on the balcony, and wave, before sliding back down to more onlookers for whom $1, $5, or $20 were no big deal to part with. Climbing was a better choice than performing her gymnastics ground routine in the Bourbon Street juice of beer, vomit, urine, and more.

It wasn't out of question for Cookie to pull in $100s over a couple hours. Got to the point that she began to get food for her little sisters and brother, which did not go over well with her mama, whose hair business was often slow. The kids had to eat it all up, no leftovers in the fridge, because the baby had a knack for not closing the door, and the roaches would scurry in to devour it.

"Why you walkin' funny?" her mama asked one day.

"I don't know what you mean," Cookie replied, but

the older woman, who had over 100-pounds advantage, got the child to the ground, sat on her, and pulled off Cookie's left shoe to reveal the hidden bankroll.

"You down bad, you little ho!" was all the young entrepreneur heard before she was physically thrown out of the house. At least she landed on grass rather than atop the trash that was regularly thrown out of the second-floor window.

Promise Home became Cookie's new home, and Elijah her biggest fan. He didn't have cash or cookies, but he made rating signs numbered "5" to "10" to judge her for gymnastic routines, and he didn't ever hold up the "5" other than as a bluff.

After Maya met Felipe and better understood the benefit of his unique skills, it was a simple matter for Elijah to also push for the benefit of bringing Cookie and Nevaeh into the fold.

Nevaeh had been accustomed to wearing an array of hoods, cowls, or veils to hide the ugly scar across her left cheek, but she soon realized it was unnecessary with Maya's group.

No one was going to clown her by saying, "Nevaeh's' Spanish for scar," "Nevaeh got 2 mouths," "Don't matter what you say about me. At the end of the day, you still ugly," or, "Nevaeh so dark, her face look like they cut up midnight." She'd heard it all and hurt from it all.

The blemish across her cheek paled in comparison to the jagged disfigurement across her heart.

Maya sensed it. Nevaeh was the only one she let practice with the razor-sharp ninja stars. Showed her moves with the knife beyond a simple thrust. How to move with her weapon so they were one and the same. How to use a blade to keep an opponent at a distance instead of solely focusing on tight jabs to wound.

"You're like me," Nevaeh said one day to Maya. "People underestimate us based on what they see. Or we scare them. But we're stronger than they realize."

Nevaeh added, "Stronger inside, I mean."

"We all are," said Maya.

Maya only needed Elijah to go solo and take a large enough bag with him for a necessary field trip errand up to City Park, but he convinced her otherwise Tuesday morning.

"If Cookie, Felipe, and Nevaeh come with me, then we can each have smaller bags. Less likely to attract attention."

"That sounds like a good idea, Elijah," Maya agreed. "No cutting up. Be back by nightfall, okay?"

Maya knew he wanted to hang with his friends. Why not let kids be kids? Their childhood had been taken from them. Let them enjoy a warm December day together.

5 Cold & Bold

Step two, on a Wednesday, felt less random for those on the list, exactly as it was supposed to be. Vinh Nguyen owned the long falling-apart building on St. Bernard, a few blocks outside of the French Quarter.

"Sister Pat, repeat that," he ordered.

"Fucking hell, Vinnie. I'm standing on the sidewalk. Health inspector put us out," she said erratically as if on uneven drugs, before taking a drag on her cigarette.

"Explain yourself. This makes no sense," he rumbled.

Sister Pat winced. "He said it was a mandatory closure. Too many critical violations."

"A what?"

"Until we correct some things."

"Why didn't you give him the envelope?" Nguyen fussed.

"Vinnie," Sister Pat tried, "This wasn't on our regular inspection schedule. I tried to give him cash from the drawer, but he shrugged it off."

"An honest health inspector!"

"I know. What's the world coming to? Here's the critical violation list."

Nguyen was furious. "He wouldn't let you correct them on the spot?!"

"No, Vinnie. We got cited for, 1. Food prepared on premises and held under refrigeration was not disposed of after seven days, 2. Rusty grill, 3. Improper dishwashing equipment, 4. Flies and roaches present, 5. Food services and utensils unclean to sight and touch, 6. Um…"

"What?"

She huffed and continued reading from the paper she held with disdain, "6. No food safety certificate held by owner or designated employee."

"Sister Pat. We go way back. Many years. I tell everyone *cục vàng* you are. Special person. You are not the owner. You are who?"

"The manager," she said reluctantly.

"Mmm hmm," he replied, "Which is another word for designated employee."

"Vinnie, I haven't had that certificate since the day we opened in 1998."

"Get it. I want my restaurant opened immediately."

"There's more…"

"Sister Pat, what have you not told me?"

"They shut down the grocery store too. All the black mold in the ceiling tiles."

"What the fuckity fuck! That's been there since Hurricane Katrina!"

Even sitting in his boat and casting for redfish steps from his hideaway fishing camp house on the way down to the Gulf of Mexico couldn't calm down Vinh Nguyen.

This task had been an easy one for Cookie. Scouting it out meant buying a candy bar at so-called Majestic Supermarket and eating 3-pounds worth of spicy boiled crawfish at Southern Seafood, looking around to see both places full of code violations, and delivering the $5,000 bribe herself.

The health inspector Jim Edwards officially made a $52,000 salary, but all the bribes over the years afforded him both Covington and Destin homes.

Felipe had a more challenging task, though he relished this kind of thing. After getting the word from Ayana about the layout at T-Boy's place, he was ready.

"Bet, his keys and wallet on the couch?"

"That's where he dropped them," she said.

Felipe asked, "What about phone?"

"Hmm," she said. "That's a trickier move. The night I was there, it was on the bed."

"Piece of cake," he smiled.

"Felipe, be careful," she warned. "He's really big."

"Thanks, but I got this."

Felipe staked out T-Boy's apartment from the overgrown 1-lot park a few doors down. A lot of people would find this the tedious part of the job. Not Felipe. Sitting, waiting, and thinking was fine with him.

He recalled growing up in Panama City. Barrio Chino on a rough block of Calle Carlos Mendoza where the street filled with water when it rained. Walking under the Chinese gate a block away to see tourists at Mercado de Mariscos across Cinta Costera. Wishing his familia could also be so carefree. Mama working long hours. Eduardo's nonstop studying. Luis thieving. As for Felipe, he was always working in San Felipe Neri market or hustling up tours to visitors who loved to take photos of the dilapidated colonial buildings. Somehow seeing beauty in what Felipe only knew as sadness.

Emigrating to the U.S. when his oldest brother Eduardo got a full ride School of Architecture scholarship to Tulane University and eventually brought the three others in the family across the water. Hard working mindset served Felipe well in New Orleans, a city where a half-Chinese Panamanian fit in the mix. At least until Luis got him kicked out of the house.

"ADST," he said quietly. "Ads, sad, sat, tad," he came up with.

"PIME," was next and he continued on. This was a pastime Felipe did as a kid who felt like an only child. Luis wouldn't have anything to do with him. He played Scrabble once, so he thought, why not play it in his mind?

Felipe went through several rounds before a car pulled up around 2:00 AM The large man who got out was clearly T-Boy. Felipe studied the house's windows, watched the inside illumination, checked his watch, and waited.

About 45 minutes later, darkness. Felipe checked his watch again and continued to wait for another half hour to be safe. The job would be easy, but as with anything in life, timing was everything.

"Don't need any of the tools in my backpack," he said to himself when he saw the cheap doorknob. Took an already-bent paper clip out of his pocket and went to work. In a matter of seconds, Felipe was in. He quietly closed the door almost all the way in case of needing a quick exit while making it clear the door wasn't open.

Next, he briefly closed his eyes to adjust to the darkness. There would be no flashlight used tonight. Maya had shown him how to maneuver his way without stumbling into something that would wake a sleeping T-Boy.

The couch was within steps of the door. Felipe ran his hand along the cushion until he came to what were clearly keys and wallet. Left them there. Didn't want keys jingling along the way.

The challenge was to come. Felipe made his way based on the layout Ayana had drawn, counting his steps the way Maya had taught him, and soon enough he was there.

First, he felt across the dresser just in case. No luck. The big man was snoring, so that helped. Felipe started at the foot of the bed and slipped his hand along the outer part of it all the way up to the headboard. Nothing.

T-Boy's back was to him.

"Here we go," thought Felipe, who got to the floor, and crawled around to the other side. Again, he began at the foot end and slowly moved forward while his right hand swept across for T-Boy's phone.

The closer he got to the other end, the closer he would be to T-Boy's head. Felipe took a deep pull of air and began to breath solely through his nose as he inched along. Still no phone.

He could almost feel the air from T-boy's snoring when his left hand bumped up against the phone on the floor. Before picking it up, he slowly slid it across the hardwood floor until it was underneath him, so that picking it up wouldn't cause a sudden light.

Suddenly T-Boy turned over, and Felipe felt his heart jump through his chest They weren't face to face, but it was close. He paused, but in seconds the snoring continued. Felipe kept from a sigh of relief. A short time after, he was out the front door, making sure to lock it, with keys, wallet, and phone in hand.

"Yes, yes, yes," he whispered and ran at top speed,

feeling sparkling bravery all the way to the uppermost point of the Claiborne Bridge. Following instructions, he tossed all three items into the waters of the Industrial Canal.

Compared to this and what she'd experienced at T-Boy's place, Ayana had a far simpler task to accomplish later that night. As predictable as could be, Flora Mosley and her friend/roommate/drug runner companion Brit, were out partying.

Ayana watched them zoom off, clearly all dolled up for the night.

"This feels like nothing compared to what Zachary and Elijah are doing, but that's all good," she said while walking into the building.

A little Pomerian ran up barking ferociously at her when she entered the condo. Ayana was prepared with a needle, and she quickly reached down to pop the ruff at the back of its neck with a sedative. He carried on for a bit more but soon calmed down.

"Of course," she said to the "Bad Bitch" pink neon sign prominently mounted above a large mirror. In fact, most of what she saw, aside from the general disarray, was a temple to ego and shallowness.

This was a place where wreaking havoc would be child's play, but Ayana was a team player, so she kept to Maya's instructions. The two of them were the closest in age of the group, and over the past few years they'd become like sisters.

That only went so far, though. It wasn't that Maya came across as acting above everyone else. She was friendly and kind. It's that she was living with a weight, a sense of duty, and a need for occasional isolation. All of this and immeasurable skills gave her a sense of otherworldly mystery.

Throughout her time living with the group, Ayana was commuting to her job at the Tulane University biomedical lab. Zachary was also out and around New Orleans, and the two of them served as Maya's eyes and ears for the state of things in the city.

Ayana had cooked up this particular recipe in the lab. First, she put on gloves and a mask, then went to each bathroom, pulled the sink stopper, tossed in makeup and as many beauty items as would fit, filled the basin 3/4 full of water. Next, she added Sodium Hydroxide, listening to the hiss as it reacted with the water. Only a few drops so the water didn't boil and produce steam. Next, to be petty, she waited a bit before adding a few more drops. This time it was Hydrogen Sulfide for that perfect rotten egg smell.

She knew that the two chemicals could serve to neutralize each other, controlling the corrosion from the former or the smell from the latter. For that reason, she released the drops of Hydrogen Sulfide at the edge of each sink basin.

"This feels like a prank," she grumbled. "But I get it. Save big moves for the big players on the list. Step one was disruption staged to appear anonymous. Step two was a clear, "We're messing with you. Now you wonder what comes next," repeating Maya's words to them.

Nevaeh and Lil Bit handled their roles from outside the house in the woods. Hours after Ayana returned, they took turns with a throwaway phone and an app that would allow them to both call from a separate, temporary, disposable 504 number. Their scripts however were identical.

With a proper-voiced fearful whisper, "Please help. My parents aren't home yet. There's a man in the house with a gun. I don't know how he got in. Maybe the back door. You've got to help. Please." Such histrionics that the other had to be in another place during each call.

Both Nevaeh and Lil Bit made it clear they were locked in the second-floor bathroom and affected a rushed scared sense of this false evil, while clearly stating and repeating the exact address. Nevaeh went first on Maya's assumption that an Orleans Parish 911 call would take longer to respond to than that of Jefferson Parish. It was still the case that Lil Bit's call got quicker action. Three JPSO squad cars hightailed it to Sena between West Esplanade and Veterans, pulling in front of the largest house on the block by far. The officers immediately ran to the door, though one of them sensed something not quite right.

A few sharp swings with the battering ram were all it took before the frenzied men ran inside, guns drawn, to the sight of Louis Rizzo Jr. sprawled out on the couch. One hand grasped a piece of pizza. The other was down his sweatpants while porn played on the large screen TV. The volume was low since family was upstairs sleeping.

"What the hell?!" as he jolted into attention and added, "Nate?"

"Lou?" responded one of the officers before yelling, "Guns down! Guns down! This is my boy, Lou Rizzo. It's his house."

While everyone caught their collective breath for a moment, Mafia underboss Louis Rizzo Sr. skipped down the stairs, shotgun leading the way.

"Whoa. Whatta you think you're doin'?" he growled. "Okay, Lou?"

"Yeah, dad."

"Turn that shit off before your mother and sister see it," the elder pointed at the screen before shaking his head at the officers and saying, "I moved from Kenner for this?"

Three and a half miles away, closer to the lake, a lone NOPD squad car raced up Marconi before barreling down Swan. The vehicle looked like what it had been through, but the sirens worked well.

The two officers ran up the walkway, cutting between a manicured lawn and shrubs. Seconds after their battering ram broke the door open, and they looked around to see nothing happening on the first floor, they were met with a piercing security alarm.

"How could somebody break in if..." started one of them.

"Tommy, that you?"

Louder. "I said, Tommy, that you?"

The NOPD officers saw a steely eyed Anthony Rizzo stride down the staircase in a plush-looking bathrobe over pinstripe pajamas. He had no gun. Didn't need one. Bit his lip. Tommy, his son, hadn't gotten home yet.

Rizzo narrowed his eyes. Pointed his right index finger while his hands shook with rage.

"You. Get Gretchen on the phone. Now."

"Sorry, sir. We didn't realize someone was swatting

you," tried the officer.

"Shut your trap. Phone."

To himself, "I can't believe I moved back from Slidell."

While Police Chief Gretchen Winters was groveling to the man whose family had run New Orleans, the surrounding parishes, and plenty of the state for the better part of a century, Elijah and Zachary were across the lake.

Northwest of Madisonville, in a new subdivision called Songbird Court, they had passed streets named House Finch, Downy Woodpecker, and Pine Warbler on their way to the new street with a house under construction.

"Great Egret. Here it is," said Elijah.

"Naming the streets after all the birds they eliminate. Classy," added Zachary.

"Dang, you're cynical."

The older man shrugged. They'd been there once before to scout it out. He didn't like it then either.

They both pulled their T-shirts to up over their heads to fully cover themselves with makeshift masks, as shown by Maya. In case of cameras. License plate had been covered since before they turned off Highway. 22.

Both walked to a house that was almost identical to all the others they passed along the way. Both took collapsible batons from their backpacks, broke lower windowpanes on different sides, and cleared out all the glass before pouring a full gallon of gasoline across the windowsills and into the house. Tossed the gas cans in too.

Both Elijah and Zachary had long grill lighters that they used to torch the outer part of the windowsills. As the flames spread quickly to the inside, they tossed the lighters in too.

"That's for Aunt Nekisha!" yelled Elijah.

Zachary immediately ran over to him.

"Shut up. Whatta you doin'? Neighbors gonna hear you."

Elijah stared at him stubbornly. "So. I got nobody."

"You got all of us. A family. Maya loves you."

"Nah," Elijah shook his head. "She's 'bout to be gone too. I'm not mad at her. Maya gotta do what she gotta do. Can't make me like it, though."

"C'mon," Zachary tried.

"Sometimes I can tell what's gonna happen in the future. I've seen Maya laying on her back with snow all around her. A few times"

"In New Orleans? Stop playin'."

Over the past few years, the two of them had gotten close while Zachary showed Elijah how to do research for Maya. Using the Orleans Parish assessor's website, the Louisiana state corporation database, searching liquor license lists, checking LLCs, and using two disparate pieces of information to open up a new world of knowledge.

Zachary had also gotten Elijah into authors like Chester Himes, Walter Mosley, Robert Deane Pharr, Donald Goines, John Edgar Wideman, and others. Tonight, though, there was jagged tension between them.

Mayor Rosalind Elloie and Rizzo attorney Nick Noto's phones were more than busy the next day.

6 Everything Must Change

New Orleans lived by vendetta. The ancient Sicilian code of silence to police permeated the city ever since the Italians came by boat in the 1800s. You handle it yourself. Even before this, though, New Orleans was a city where men would duel to handle matters.

I'm not doing anything that hasn't already been happening for a good long time. I read in a book, back when I could see with my eyes, that 200 years ago there were more duels here than anywhere in the world. Imagine that. And the population wasn't even 50,000 back then. Vendettas are what perpetuate the cycle, right? Whether for honor, tradition, or a big payback, what some call getting your lick back. It can be fuzzy where vendetta ends and simple revenge begins, though.

To me, people are so closely linked in New Orleans that it doesn't have to be an ongoing family blood feud to be a vendetta. If it adds links to an unbroken unending chain, it's part of the perpetual city vendetta.

I remember a few years back when there was a shooting outside a beloved restaurant up on Canal St. The streets said that young man A who got shot was hit because his brother B left the shooter's C friend D in a burned-out car in the East. That happened due to D's killing his secret lover E, who had a big mouth, so word didn't get out he was on the down low. Plus, a certain drug dealer F wanted E gone for sneaking his stash. Truth be told, the only reason E was desperate enough to do something so stupid was because G shot up E's roommate H over a card game before rent and his jacked-up car note were due, so E needed the money. Word was D took out E with the switch E himself was planning to use on G. Why did B take out D for killing E? Because B's girlfriend I was E's cousin. Quite an alphabet and only the beginning.

That's what the streets say anyway.

It's grimy, but so is New Orleans.

Reality is that some things are forgivable and others aren't. Some people can be forgiven and others can't. Plus, as far as I'm concerned, other family members have no onus to bear for what someone else did.

That's why my list has six on it, not 60. The six directly behind the deaths of my parents Franklin and Eugenia, plus Aunt Nekisha.

This is my vendetta. It ends with me, though. No more chain. The seven in my group won't be included in this part. They were the ninjas to get in and out discreetly. Set the stage with seemingly random step one events to disrupt the day and imbalance the minds of the six on the list.

Two days later, step two pulled off disruptions that were clearly not random. Enough to get them to wonder, "What's next? Who's behind it? When and where will it happen again? Why was it pulled off?"

All of them—Elijah, Cookie, Felipe, Lil Bit, Nevaeh, Ayana, and Zachary—they were great ninjas. Learned how to improvise. To use shower curtain hooks as brass knuckles, books as weapons, and all the rest. Took to their training. Followed instructions. Executed the moves. But this vendetta is mine. I'm the assassin. This isn't for them. Step three begins tomorrow. It's mine. The group meeting earlier today was what I expected. All of them banding together to try and convince me not to start working through the list. Zachary tried to claim an ethical contradiction in being a Buddhist assassin. I expected it from him.

He asked, "How can a belief system of peace stand for violence? I had two words ready. *Issatsu tashō*, Japanese for "Kill one that many may live." It's more complicated than people realize. Try and keep certain people from repeating horrible actions. There's precedent. This was carried out and organized by an unofficial Buddhist priest named Inoue Nisshō almost 100 years ago. Like Nisshō's group, mine has no name.

I told Zachary and all of them that I wasn't naive enough to think eliminating a handful of cancers on civilization was going to change things tremendously, but I knew with surety that these specific people had come to the end of their plague days.

"This doesn't feel like Zen," he said.

"It's Zen at war," I responded. "It's action," but I knew he still thought it a problem ideology. I also knew whether he thought it was a terrible Zen or not, his usual clear and evident crossroad of thought meant he would likely come around. He had dense loyalty to me and always gave me the benefit of the doubt.

"Maya, you're like a sister to me," said Ayana. "I hear you. You shaved your head, so I see you're now in warrior mode, but is there anything I can say to convince you not to follow through?"

"I'm a warrior whether I'm fighting or not," I

clarified, adding, "How will the last become first and first become last without this?" is what I responded to her. "I know," she quietly said, because she did know with her big heart. If there was a person of endless benevolence, it was Ayana.

Their concern was for me, I knew. Concern that either one of the six on the list would win their battle with me, or the vendetta would continue with the target on my back. Either way, concern that my own death was impending.

"Sifu taught us all many things in class," I explained, "but there were some things he only taught me." The others weren't ready, especially not to train themselves to accept, not fear, mortality. "That's the way of the warrior," he told me.

I was trained to think about all the ways I might die based on *The Hagakure*. Before I went to sleep, I would reflect on them. Still do. When the day comes, I will receive it. I made sure to add for Ayana's sake an aside of, "Are you saying my new hairdo's not styling?"

The tension in the air was strong. I could sense it. Each person got their turn to speak their peace and all took the time to shoot their shot at making me decide to fall back from the plans.

Except one. Elijah. "No," he responded. I tried a second time. What did he want to say? That's what it took. I knew it was coming. He was never one for glassy optimism.

"You're talking about big issues and themes and all that," he blurted out. "I might sound stupid or young or whatever, but I don't care. This is personal to me too. They killed Aunt Nekisha. I couldn't save her. It's also personal because it's you carrying this out. Those people on the list—they all deserve street justice. Got no problem with that. They won't ever end up in a courthouse. That man who had the party at his house and setting up all that stuff with kids at Promise Home, he never went to trial. People like him don't. I get the philosophy of why you're doing what you're doing. It sounds all wise and stuff. But I don't want to lose you. Y'all can say Elijah's flashing out and talking crazy, but I said what I said."

I couldn't disagree with him or anyone who expressed in their way how important the house in the woods was to them. It was no weird assumption. Just because the next step was known and necessary to me didn't mean that it wasn't also painful for me.

What I did say to Elijah and to them all was that if it was a tall ladder for them to climb to understand what and why I was carrying out the vendetta, then I was fine with that. I concluded with, "It's time for business."

They hadn't expected that for the next week I would no longer be with them, meditating, training, sleeping, and spending time together. What I needed, though, was to self-isolate before and after each of the six deaths I would commit. It went beyond the acts I would carry out. It was separation.

There was no other way I could purify myself but go deeper into the woods. After heartfelt hugs with all of them, that is what I did.

As I walked to my spot, I heard a melody and lyrics, "Everything must change. Nothing remains the same." I rubbed my hand across my head. The only other time in my life I'd shaved my head was when I was at LSU before dropping out. It was to keep the trichotillomania urges at bay. Can't pull out your own hair and chew on it if you don't have any.

I don't know what memory bump on my head was activated when I rubbed it, but I immediately remember what Felipe said at the meeting. In the lead up to all this, he had read a book about the Mafia by a man named Selwyn Raab. And, of course, he was the one to point out in front of the group that, "What's interesting about what Maya's doing is the word 'Mafia' was slang that originally meant 'acting as a protector against the arrogance of the powerful.' Now the Mafia's powerful and arrogant. Maya's the protector. She's literally Mafia taking on the Mafia."

"Felipe, go run through the woods," popped off Cookie, though I could hear the others were in agreement.

Felipe's right, though. Words matter. How they get corrupted matters. Thinking of my vendetta feels a certain way in this city. It isn't an ongoing family vs. family vendetta. I'm not going so far as to indiscriminately include other family members in it. That's where I draw the line. I told Jason Polidore that. Made it clear when I said, "It's time."

The days of the specific people are done. Vinh Nguyen, Anthony Rizzo, Louis Rizzo Sr., Joey Lyons, T-Boy, and Flora Mosley, your days are numbered. All the terrible things you've done to others or had someone else do to others end now.

There's a baldie about to be coming for you. I could die from a fire, drowning, house collapsing in a tornado, car wreck...am I hearing something?

A pause. "Is that about it?"

Maya turned her head toward Elijah. It was only the two of them for now in what would be her private new spot for the next week. He'd been writing down her words as quickly as he could. His wrist was sore, and his soul felt worse.

"Almost," she said. "You brought the bags from City Park?"

Reluctantly, "They're here."

Maya nodded. "I only have one thing left to say. Flora Mosley, you're first."

Elijah didn't see her tear up and slightly turn her head toward him as he walked away.

7 Zen At War

IF YOU ONLY PLAY TO YOUR STRENGTHS, THEN YOU DON'T improve. You don't expand. You merely stay limited. Especially if your strength is your looks, not a talent.

In a nutshell, this was the life of Flora Mosley. She didn't apply herself in school, had no interest in extracurricular activities, and shied away from her father's martial arts.

By some strange bolt of lightning, she was accepted by Texas Southern University but was one step out of there even before her father Julius Mosley's health began to fail. Her back and forth from New Orleans to Houston stopped being school related and instead turned to running drugs to the Crescent City for the Rizzo's. One big haphazard hustle.

Flora was aimless. She lived for night life. Her friends, including her sidekick Brit, were all her partying buddies. In a place like New Orleans, this wasn't anomalous.

Alcoholism was the baseline for many, and most any kind of drug was easier to find than fresh food or produce. Working with the Rizzo's was a natural step.

When her mother Samira kicked Flora out of the family house on Toledano over by the river, it was only natural that she and Brit got a place together. A condo in the Warehouse District was their mutual choice for the sake of being equidistant to wherever the bar, party, or concert was that night.

"Really, Brit?" Flora scoffed.

"Bro, it's only for a few days to help out my dad," came a sheepish tone from her phone.

"Admit it. You're freaked out about the bathroom sink thing. Period."

"Uh, and the slashed tires."

"That shit's probably on you," Flora accused. "How many one and done's did you have in the past month?"

"No, no," said Brit. "It's not on me. I fucked all those dudes at their places. You think I told them where I stay?"

"I don't know, but only a man would think to do that. Women know how expensive beauty supplies are."

Brit sighed. "It's weird. Like somebody's trying to send a message."

"Well, I got a piece in my purse if they try it again. Plus, you know I keep a blade on me."

"Doesn't everybody in New Orleans?" Britt replied.

"All I know is this," said Flora, "It would be a damn shame to get my nails done solo."

"You'll be good. Daddy's in the middle of some mess. I'm keeping the peace. That way my half of the rent stays flowing," referring to her allowance.

Flora couldn't resist a jab at her friend. "Here I thought you were turnin' tricks for that."

"Bitch, listen. Head is holy. If I charged those guys to eat my coochie, I'd be queen of New Orleans."

"Bitch, you crazy," she laughed.

"Just like you, my twin from another mother."

Flora gave up. "Alright, I'll hit you later."

After hanging up, Flora looked around her place. She wasn't going to admit it to Brit, but she had started double-checking things. Was something missing from the fridge?

Had her clothes been moved around? Was anything else off-kilter?

Knowing that someone had been in her personal sanctum had her feeling violated. She felt it had nothing to do with the flat tires two days prior. That happened all the time in New Orleans. Brit had seen the nails poking out of the tires same as she had.

On her way to the nail place on Carrollton, Flora thought about what she might do later on. There hadn't been a weekend night that she and Britt didn't party together since she could remember.

That was how they met after all. A Friday night at Cooter Brown's. Or was it Snake and Jakes? No, it must have been Ms. Mae's.

Flora had been there with friends, dancing on the bar and playing at being a stripper, as usual, while Lil Wayne's "Lollipop" was blasting. What did her hazy eyes see across the room but another woman doing the same thing.

In some cases like this, an alpha will seek to assert and establish dominance. Flora and Brit were different. They both recognized kindred spirits and the power of doing their thing together.

Not only were they as conjoined as individuals could be, people told them all the time that their voices sounded almost identical. They thought that was hilarious because Flora had attended McMain, while you better believe Councilman Jim Casimir got Brit in at Newman.

Flora spent her time at the nail salon fruitlessly reaching out to others for where the move was that night. She was frustrated, muttering "Flora Fucking Mosley shouldn't have to stoop to this." Eventually she finished and returned home.

There her future ended and past began.

Maya knew two things—that Flora would be armed, with a weapon in her purse, and that Flora running her mouth would allow Maya to know precisely where she was at.

There was another advantage. Though she was blind, no one on the list knew it.

"Gotta keep it that way," she said to herself while she waited, touching both the red Buddha pendant hanging from her neck and the prayer beads around her wrist that served as her personal battle flags. Flora's yapping dog was already taken care of the same way that Ayana had handled it.

It was a scant few minutes before Maya heard a key in the lock and the doorknob turned. She waited long enough for Flora to step in and make a 180 to close the door. It put her right shoulder with designer purse closest to Maya. As Maya was moving toward her, recalling their heights were similar, she heard Flora gasp in surprise. Maya reached for her shoulder with both hands, felt a leather strap, and pulled it down quickly, turning off to her right.

"Bitch!" Flora yelled as Maya angled her body and delivered a low left kick to Flora's upper ankle. There was a reason for this, which became clear when Maya threw Flora's purse across the room. The impact caused the vibrator inside to flip on its switch at the highest level of speed. It shook inside the purse, gradually worked its way out, and slowly wiggled across the hardwood floor.

Flora's anger increased exponentially. An intruder.

Maya Gaines, no less. "You!" she let loose. "Now I see. The flat tires. My bathroom sink. That shit was you," as she squared up with Maya, who feinted with her left and right while she moved in open diamond footwork.

"Better believe it," Maya said.

"You dumb ho. You know I'm going to kill you, right?" blustered Flora. She snuck a peek to see if she could dash to her purse. Her pink Glock 48 was in it, and the switch was on in the back to turn the pistol into a machine gun to chop down Maya. Knife was in the purse too.

"This is it for you, Flora," Maya responded without a hint of emotion before she quickly bounded forward and popped Flora to her right ear with the tiger claw jab. They both knew Maya was a better fighter by far.

"Fuckkk!" Flora hollered before adding, "I thought you lived by a code and all that dumb shit."

This ironically reminded Maya of what Flora's father Sifu Julius Mosley had said. "The strongest opponent is the one who is serious and at ease, not the one loud and acting a fool."

They both shifted, positioning themselves, as Maya said, "You mean what I got from Sifu? Who you lied on me about. I would never poison him. Or start a fire. You know they killed my Aunt Nekisha?"

"Why aren't you going after them then?" Flora used her words to trick so she could grab random Mardi Gras beads, lunge forward, and run to tackle Maya.

Flora put Maya on her back and knocked the door wide open while she did it. After being momentarily stunned, Maya realized this proximity to Flora was even better.

Blows rained down on Maya as the cheap beads were swung at her, but she used her arms to block them, spun out of the way, and fired her own fist shots at Flora before pulling back.

Maya had something to say.

"I know what you did."

"Bitch, you don't know anything," said Flora.

"You know," said Maya. "Just like you know Tiny Brown." She also knew that Flora's eyes were showing she was registering that name. She added, "Same Tiny Brown whose sister Deja's doing a bid in the federal pen. Aliceville, Alabama. You paid Tiny to have Deja put a hit on my mom."

Flora tried to wildly swing her head side to side to accompany her now-raspy, "No, no, no."

Maya had the advantage on her as Flora moved into defensive position close to the doorway. The scene was interrupted by a different voice. This time it came from the hallway with concern in it, as if Maya was the one losing the fight.

"Maya?" wondered Nevaeh, with her knife leading the way as she entered the room. That was enough for Maya to pause in surprise, allowing Flora to elbow Nevaeh in the head and grab the knife, as the young girl crumpled to the ground.

"Now it's on," said Flora, still unknowing that her foe was blind. Though Maya couldn't see what had happened, she knew that a knife was Nevaeh's primary weapon. This would test her.

Maya had prepared with shades, tight clothes, and

cowl—all in black—plus a small bag, but she hadn't expected one of her group to show up.

"Ayana must have told her where the condo was," she thought and added a loud, "Come on, Flora. What you got? Sifu poured everything into me since you were nothing but a disappointment."

"Shut up!" hissed Flora.

"He told me," Maya said. "How it made him sad to have a such a disappointment as a daughter."

"Shut the fuck up!"

Maya's technique was to elevate Flora's anger since it's the worst state of mind for an effective fighter. She also had to respect Flora's benefit of sight.

Maya counted on right-handed Flora holding the knife how most would. Not at head level, in a ridiculous way. Not as low as waist level either. Likely right at chest height or a hair below it.

They both cautiously moved around each other until Maya took a gamble after a sharp cut across her knuckles. She stepped in and began to swing high with her right, knowing that would lead Flora upward. Instead of trying to connect, she pulled her arm back as she was spinning to the left, sinking down low as she could, and extending her right foot hard in the vicinity of Flora's shins.

"Unnnh," called out Flora as Maya made contact and the knife rattled into the ground. Maya heard the sound and picked it up. Nevaeh's blade found its taste at last when Maya punctured Flora's lungs quickly from the back. One cut would have done it, but this was personal. Maya's soul joined the blade and another strike finished Flora. The trembling pain lasted for less than five minutes, then nothing.

Before Maya brought Nevaeh back to consciousness and left, she grabbed the Spanish Moss from her bag, placed it on Flora's back, and briefly meditated on what had happened.

8 The Bones Fly

Well before the news stories ran about Flora Mosley's grisly death, Maya held an impromptu meeting of the group.

"You all need to let me handle what I need to handle," she stressed.

Nevaeh shrunk. "I'm sorry. It's not Ayana's fault. She didn't know what I was going to do with the info. I just thought..."

Maya was struck by something she hadn't considered.

"Did you come to stop me or help me?"

No answer was forthcoming.

"Nevaeh?"

The younger girl rubbed her scar as a habit when put on the spot. She was going at it vigorously.

"I wanted to be by your side," she tried.

Maya threw up her hands.

"Do the rest of you feel that way? I'm not up for this because of my blindness?"

The silence was deafening again until Elijah blurted out "Can you blame us? Let us be a part of it. If we..."

"No!"

Maya rarely raised her voice.

"Use your ears and hear me. This is my vendetta. You each carried out your roles well, but your part in it is done. Do you understand?"

A few murmurs.

I said, "Do? You? Understand?"

"Yes," they all reluctantly responded.

"I'm trying to protect you all," she said. "You trying to protect me will only put yourselves in danger and make it harder for me."

"I'm sorry, Maya," said Nevaeh. "You're right."

Maya stood up.

"I'm going to the woods to do what I should've been doing half an hour ago."

As anyone in New Orleans service industry knows, the weekend is work time, not play time. Save the fun for Tuesdays and Wednesdays. Kantrell Teed, known as T-Boy since he was in grade school, was in that group. T-Boy had been an All-State football player for Carver. Accolades and scholarships. A bright future. Family counting on the money. Daddy proud. Mama proud. Until he was out with his guy Darrell who wanted to cop some coke and blues at Sean's Bar, a wild spot on Desire by the Florida Canal. T-Boy made the mistake of holding the drugs for Darrell since no one would mess with him while they hung at the bar for a bit.

That happened to be the night NOPD came through because of the shootout two days prior. The one that started in Sean's and went under houses in the next block. T-Boy met Buchi in OPP. That's how he ended up working security at the underground fights Buchi put on for Joey Lyons.

Buchi went to the Federal pen over the parties and underground fighting, but the powers that be recycled T-Boy in another location. There was always a place for 6'4" 275-pound perpetually pissed off man. No one had been proud of him for years, though.

T-Boy was extra surly because of trying to exist in the world without his wallet, phone and most of his keys. House key was it for the moment, and his landlord had fussed about providing the replacement.

"Come on. Step up," he said to the group of three sheepish men. They were from Ocean Springs, MS, never visited New Orleans before, and they'd made their way to Bourbon for some action.

King Club promised exactly that with its neon signs showing a nude woman in silhouette. So did the three women standing just off the sidewalk while they beckoned to passers-by sauntering down the street. A curled index finger with eye contact typically did the trick. New Orleans sold seduction but often delivered disenchantment.

"Come on," T-Boy growled again, annoyed while the barker/doorman was out back doing a bump with two of the dancers. T-Boy's preferred domain was not feeling like in a fishbowl out on the sidewalk. Kids drumming on buckets, a snake lady, someone's granny sashaying around, and a variety show of hustlers, vagrants, and local good timers either milling about or acutely watching the tourists in search of an easy mark.

"If I look it, I don't have to be it," was T-Boy's mantra. He'd been wearing a shirt at least a size too small to accentuate his physique for years, but since working in the Quarter, he'd grown a goatee and started shaving his head. Look tough and you don't need to act.

This particular Saturday was one where he only had to look it except for one instance. A dancer was trying to upsell a customer in the middle of private dances, got mad when he declined, and stomped off. The enraged Scott from Ocean Springs chased her downstairs before T-Boy kept them both in check while the manager mediated the situation.

"Diamond, put 'em down!" said T-Boy, referring to the stage shoes with 8-inch heels she held at ready to ferociously puncture eyes. Even after the manager walked away with the customer and it was solely the two of them, she was still drugged and riled up.

"You do the same shit every night. Damn," he said to the air smelling of cheap perfume around him once Diamond stomped to the back. It had become comical to him that any of the dancers were considered desirable. He only knew them as big pains in the ass. Except for Virgo and Big K. No mess ever with them.

Hours later, Bourbon Street was still popping, but King Club flipped off the music. On came the lights, which killed the feel immediately. 4:00 AM sharp.

"You don't gotta go home…or your hotel, but you gotta get the hell up out of here," announced the DJ. The dancers began to reluctantly tip out. Within a short period of time, T-Boy began to walk dancers to their cars.

It wasn't so busy this time of year between the holidays. Few conventions were booked two weeks out from Christmas.

It was about an hour and a half before sunrise when T-Boy trudged from the car that brought him to his front door. Shook his head. They were down bad for having architects design fancy versions of New Orleans houses after Katrina while building them so shabbily they were falling apart.

"Not just them," he muttered and added, "Damn

landlord." T-Boy meant "slumlord" because that's really what it was. He went days without electricity working in the heart of summer and winter, because Marquise fiddled with it himself to save money. That also applied to plumbing and every other issue too.

Marquise did a shoddy job and took his sweet time to show up and do it too. Always when he knew T-Boy would be at work. Marquise Accra was beloved by some in New Orleans as a rapper who was known to hold protests in the middle of the street right as Mardi Gras parades were rolling. He wasn't speaking out on the suspect origins of Mardi Gras itself or the litany of local issues but instead on international politics.

Simply put, Marquise' contradictions extended to him being a public revolutionary but a private slumlord. His name itself was also a facade. Tarius Smith wanted something that spoke of royalty in Ghana. Even had it officially changed once he had an extra few $100 handy from a jewelry scam.

"My good brother," T-Boy scoffed, thinking of how Marquise would always address him. "Psssh—all skin folk ain't kinfolk."

He stepped up to the door, key in hand. Inserted, turned, pushed. He'd done that 1,000 times before, but this time the door didn't budge.

"What?" Was he so tired he hadn't actually unlocked it or did this replacement key not work? Yes, it went in, the doorknob turned, but the door wouldn't open, even as he slowed down methodically. He didn't have a new phone yet to call Marquise.

All of a sudden, the quick sound of air prefaced

something striking his right shoulder blade. It came fast, it hit hard, and it crushed bone.

"Aaaaah!" he cried out as he reached back at the point of impact. Nothing there but throbbing pain. No question his scapula was broken.

T-Boy spun around. All he could see was a shadowy figure poised for violence. The city's security light hadn't worked since he'd been there.

This time he caught the flash of movement before, pop, his left knee was struck, and he was in severe pain in two spots.

"What the fuck?!" he cried out.

Next the side of his right knee. A glancing blow didn't feel any better. T-Boy was in agony. He limped forward.

"I'm gonna kill you!" he said.

For the first time, another voice broke the silence.

"You're the only one dying tonight, T-Boy." Calm. Matter of fact.

"Who the fuck is...wait...wait," as he slowly inched forward. "This is Maya, right? Bitch, when I get my hands on you."

This time the impact spun across his ribs from left to right before sweeping back across hard and strong from right to left."

"Aaaaah, shit!"

Maya was now standing about 7-feet away from T-Boy. She held a 9-link chain whip with a 4-inch lead weight on the end of it, which had been used to repeatedly strike T-Boy while still keeping distance.

Before he got home, she had been busy. Maya knew the apartment layout from Ayana and Felipe. She broke in, pushed his couch firmly up against the front door, shoved a table against that, and went out through a window. Then she lay in wait, same as Felipe had.

Inside would be far too confining for the chain whip to swing, plus T-Boy's size and strength would be a much larger factor. She needed space and to strike first.

T-Boy winced as he inched ahead, feeling his bones gnashing against each other. He tried to distract her with his words.

"Why are you doing this? Unnnh!"

Though the strike connected with his fleshy left forearm, it still stung and stopped him in his tracks. He didn't realize that his speech was a cue to guide Maya exactly where to aim toward.

"Why? You know why I'm here."

"Because I locked you in that room your first day at the warehouse?" he tried.

Maya recalled her inaugural fight in the warehouse under the Danziger Bridge. T-Boy made her initially think that she was there to be raped, not to fight. His kind of humor.

"Keep guessing. Here's a clue. I would've already gotten Glen Moore if cancer didn't first."

T-Boy was struck immediately, but this time by a memory, not by the chain whip.

"No, no, no, no, no. I was drinking with Arv when Glen did that."

"Did what?"

"What he did. I told him not to."

"No, you didn't. You were seen by my neighbor getting out of Glen's truck with him. Both of you had firebombs.”

T-Boy switched tactics, reverting to belligerence.

“Yeah, and Arv sat waiting in the truck. That’s all in the past. Get over it.”

For good measure, Maya sent a quick strike higher. T-Boy’s left jaw was the recipient.

“Fuccck!” he howled and rasped.

“Killing my Aunt Nekisha is unforgivable.”

Maya began to spin the chain whip to build up speed before she swung directly for T-Boy’s head, but she unexpectedly ended up on her stomach. T-Boy’s neighbor Devontre from across the street had heard the yelling, came outside, and tackled Maya. Though Devontre hadn’t played JV football for decades, he still put her down sharply.

“I gotcha, T,” he said. “Check this out,” he added as he held up Maya’s weapon.

“Ohh shit. My brother,” praised T-Boy, speaking as best he could while trying not to move his jaw. “I gotta get to the hospital. This bitch broke me the fuck up. But first we’re throwing her ass in the canal.”

They both thought that Devontre’s tackle had knocked out Maya. She hadn’t budged and didn’t say a word. Not even a moan of pain. But she was waiting and listening.

Neither man saw Maya raise up to her knees before she grabbed Devontre’s left ankle tightly while she shoved him hard with her right hand. This took him face first into T-Boy’s broken ribs and onto the ground as T-Boy pushed him off and roared in pain.

Maya avoided T-Boy’s lunge at her, grabbed her chain whip, held it closer to the lead weight at the end since space was tight, before she made her strikes to his head count.

"My war isn't with you. Go home," she said to Devontre after taking out a handful of Spanish Moss and placing it on T-Boy. As before, Maya briefly meditated on T-Boy's death before retrieving her bo staff, letting the chain whip drop into the hollowed-out bamboo, and screwing on the top part before she walked off.

Devontre's friend for the night, who was watching it all from a second-floor window, cursed at Maya and threw bathroom supplies at her.

Toothpaste, soap, lotion, and an unwrapped fast-food cheeseburger flew through the sky.

9 Turn The Lights Off

"Nicky, look. They're in a high-risk line of work. I don't mean to be insensitive, but you know. Shit happens."

"Check this out, Lou. I called my NOPD guy to get the scoop. What the news wasn't telling us."

"I respect you. Nicky, love you as a brother. Yes, the two deceased were our employees, but we got 1,000s of people on the payroll. It's a fuckin' delicate assumption I gotta be broken up about all of 'em."

"I'm aware of that, but, Lou, this is different. Both T-Boy and Flora had Spanish Moss put on them. By the killer."

"Spanish Moss, Spanish Moss? The stuff hangin' outta trees?"

"Yeah."

"What kind of voodoo shit's goin' on?"

"I don't know, Lou. But I thought you should know."

Louis Rizzo Sr. thought for a moment before posing a vacant suggestion to the family attorney Nick Noto, "Called Tony?"

"He's got that meeting about what's been happening after the guns leave the port."

"Right, right," said Rizzo. "Our too-loud Middle Eastern partners."

"Well, the kids who work for them, but yes."

"Nicky, whose neck's on the line? Theirs or the guy who lives down the block, walks over to work, and takes stupid pictures to impress his little friends on social media? Buck's gotta stop with those who make the real money."

"I understand, Lou. Kids are different now. Documenting themselves holding money and machine guns. Definition of dumb."

"Dumb and dumber. There's only two rules. It's never changed," emphasized Rizzo. "Don't snitch and never talk about business."

Noto let loose his sigh. "They don't know how the game is played. But our people haven't run the corner stores for decades. I agree that our business partners need to see the seriousness of this."

"You said a mouthful. We started this shit. Used to be mostly Sicilians. Now it's the fuckin' United Nations out there."

Noto knew this was also referring to the Rizzo family involvement with the Chinese and Mexican drug cartels who had made major inroads in the U.S., but he changed the subject. His wife was Greek.

"How's the family doing after that JP mishap?"

"Mishap? They came in guns blazin'. Woulda shot Lou's pecker off if I hadn't got downstairs in time. JPSO. The people I pay taxes to keep me safe. Tony had the same thing happen in Lakeview. Somebody's fuckin' with us, Nick. Joey Lyons had a house under construction get torched."

"I heard they drowned Vinnie's jewelry store in the East too."

"At this point, I'm not happy about none of it. Conspiracies, though? Not buying it. Who'd come after the Rizzo's? Dumbest thing I ever heard of."

"I don't feel good about all this stuff, Lou, but alright. Be safe."

"I'll look both ways before I cross the fuckin' street. Later."

Rizzo's son, Louis Jr., was upstairs on the phone finishing up his own call with friend and business partner Joey Lyons, who was poolside at his home on the North Shore. Too cold to swim, but he wanted to drink and smoke.

"Dar's mad. We were supposed to go to Miami this weekend. Warmest place in the country right now. Like it's my fault a new build got turned into a campfire?"

"Something's off. All this happening at the same time," said Rizzo. "My dad's not worried about it, though."

"Maybe he should be," said Joey. "They got me even up here in God's country. Talk soon, Lou."

Joey Lyons poured another drink. Bourbon neat.

"Breakfast of champions," he proclaimed as a one-man toast and held the glass to the sky. It was almost noon. Dar was still at church, which had become a point of contention.

Before, they were holy heathens. Talking the talk but rarely walking the walk. After Nick Noto kept Joey from seeing the inside of a courtroom, Darlene, his wife, said it was a message from God, and she began attending church regularly. Not Joey. He started drinking way more than usual. His belly and blood vessels along his nose showed it.

Joey was furious that someone would have the nerve to torch a Lyons Industries home, but he wasn't hurting. Insurance would cover it. The class action lawsuits building up around the state? Not a concern. Running the largest construction company in Louisiana comes with certain privileges, and Joey knew he was protected.

So what if he didn't properly build to the intense heat and humidity of the climate, which meant the buildings were lucky to last a decade without serious issues?

So what if they paid Realtors double their usual commission to steer buyers to the shoddily-built homes and pushed Loan Officers away from their own clients? Also elbowed out the Realtors too whenever possible so they could more easily defraud the buyers.

Lyons Industries was too big to touch. Too important to the state for anything with legal legs to gain real traction. Customer service was for newbies. Following the rules was for suckers. Lyons' business was like a steamroller. So what if he didn't follow the rules?

Joey was partial to Blanton's Bourbon, especially with a cigar. Truth be told, he was perturbed that none of the new staff had come out to check on him.

"Bottle getting low. Out of salami. Popcorn too," he said shaking his head. Joey loved cheap cheddar popcorn with his drinking as much as he favored pricier cured meat.

He grabbed the wireless intercom and fired off, "Hello? Hello? I need somebody out here asap."

"These people," he muttered while he smacked the top sides of his own head with both hands slightly smashing his LSU visor down on his ears, his sunglasses strap bouncing on his neck. Joey was peeved.

No one was coming, though. Dar told the house staff to come in at 2:00 PM for payback due to him canceling the Miami trip. These were the new ones hired after the grease-on-the-floor incident led to the long-time staff getting fired.

The second reason for 2:00 PM was that Joey's other half expected to be home by then. Not from church service and lunch with "the girls." All of that had been a facade for the past three years, same as the marriage itself, as Dar complained to anyone within earshot

In actuality, Dar's claimed message from God leading her to regularly attending church was only cover for a weekly hotel appointment with a mortgage banker from Mandeville named Ed and a New Orleans woman-for-hire who went by Mercedes. Each Sunday, Mercedes would drive the Causeway with her bag of drugs and toys.

While their party commenced, Ed's wife thought he was at the AA meeting he kept promising to regularly attend after being fired from another bank for sexual harassment. Truth be told, a dissolute lifestyle had him resembling a walking cadaver at age 51, so the only way he could "get" most women was cash or employee intimidation.

Dar was twisted too, and she loved the idea of sex and drugs with an ugly wild man. Made her feel even more depraved. Add Mercedes and it was quite the opposite of holy with all three of them each Sunday morning. While Joey was poolside yelling, "Where the fuck are you?" into the intercom, the trio had hard rock music blasting as they defied gender roles.

"I love hookers!" yelled Ed. "Party!"

Mercedes clocked that and made a mental note to up her hourly to $1,200 due to annoyance.

Truth be told, Ed was quite smart and made a lot of money, but he did a poor job at reading the room, whichever room he was in. Or more so that he didn't care what people thought about his lack of evolution since the college frat days.

Joey Lyons, his counterpart in many of the ways that mattered, slammed down the intercom, and got up to go inside and give the staff a piece of his mind. He heard a rustle of bamboo and turned to see one of the trees pull backward at the top before it flipped back across toward him.

Holding onto it was a person who quickly slid down from over 20 feet up and stepped in front of the bamboo row.

"You?!" His glassy eyes popped. Even with a cowl obscuring her face, he knew. The candlelight memory from this very spot.

"It's been a few years."

They both remembered well the party Joey had in that very spot three years ago with the politicians, the big names, the escorts, and the kids that Joey was bringing in from Promise Home. Both recalled the fight with Maya and Arv, Maya winning solidly, and escaping with video evidence of the depraved actions by using the bamboo trees to pull her herself over the fence to the lawn and escape.

This time, she used the same method to get in. The same weapon she'd used to pull the bamboo down to her from across the fence was by her side. Bo staff on the lawn side, because she knew she'd be returning to it.

Maya spoke first, saying, "Considering you're a

mobbed-up business hotshot and I'm nobody, you must be thinking the odds are pretty good in your favor. To be honest, I can't disagree. At all. But I've come to learn something I can't shake. Vendetta begins in the womb. I was born for this. Today's not your lucky day."

Maya moved her wrist to begin doing figure eights with the chain whip while Joey mocked her.

"You couldn't prove anything back then. Now is no different."

"I'm not here to prove anything," Maya said as she slowly walked forward.

At this point, Joey realized that being a little tipsy, or as Dar would say, "tispy," was not in his favor.

"I got security be here quick, bitch."

"Been hearing that word a lot," while still advancing and keeping him talking.

Joey grabbed his ashtray and fired it at her. It sailed a foot over her right shoulder. Maya couldn't see it coming. He thought, stunned, "She didn't even flinch."

Maya felt it rifle past her, though, so, in response, she bobbed a little to her left and right to keep him off guard. Joey fired the empty bourbon bottle at her, but it hit the ground to her side, shattered, and skipped along.

Maya picked up the speed on her chain whip moves, taking it in a loop above and around her head.

Joey didn't know what kind of weapon she had, but he didn't want to be anywhere near it. He felt ridiculous as he kicked a beach ball at her, and it landed next to the broken glass.

"You've done a lot of lowdown stuff, but I'm here for one reason. You had my Aunt Nekisha killed."

"You're mistaken. I didn't know that she..."

"Didn't know she'd be in the house? Since you only cared about killing me? That's what you meant?"

"Wait," he protested. "That wasn't my people."

"Cut it out. T-Boy already admitted to it."

All of a sudden, the enormity of the realization hit Joey. Flora Mosley and T-Boy's deaths weren't street stuff. It made him wonder about the grease on his floors and…

"Did you have my new build home torched?"

Maya loved this. She knew exactly where he was standing.

"Yes."

She continued closer, swinging the chain whip, and softly began to sing, "Everything must change. Nothing remains the same," and repeated it again.

Joey punched the intercom in desperation mode. "Help! Help! Help me!" he called in a voice now soaked with fear. She could hear he wasn't more than 10-feet away.

Maya had one last thing to say. "This is for the kids too."

At that, he took off running toward the house like she knew he would. Maya bounded two quick jump steps forward, in case of broken glass, and let loose the chain whip. She wasn't trying to hit him. Instead, the angle she released it at sent the lead weight in front of him before she snapped her wrist to the side to wrap it around his ankle.

Maya pulled back hard. She heard the grunt as he hit the ground face first. Behind her a beach ball sat next to broken glass.

"No. No, please," he begged. Maya lightly tested with her foot to see how close they were to the water. Once she knew, she grabbed the chain whip handle with both hands and pulled fast and strong to her left, yanking Joey Lyons into his own pool.

He wasn't a strong swimmer, but he was flailing for his life. Each time he headed toward his side, Maya would move there.

"I can do this all day," Joey called out.

Felipe had come to the house a week prior for recon. Maya walked to the table where Joey had been sitting, found what she expected, and pressed a button. Not the wireless intercom but a remote control.

The pool cover groaned to life and began to hum its way across the water. Joey realized immediately that she was forcing him out. He couldn't stay under water and wait for her to leave. There wasn't enough room between the water and the cover for him to stay in the pool.

All he could do was give it one last try. He swam and splashed as fiercely as he could despite all the bourbon in his bloodstream. Got to the end. Maya or not, it was time to jump out and run for it.

He put his hands up on the side, preparing to catapult himself upward. Maya had lost her footing, fell to the ground, but recovered and looped the chain whip around his neck. She pulled up as high as her arms would reach. Joey flailed and struck her with his fists wherever he could until he breathed his last air. The pool cover had pushed up against him by that point, so Maya tossed the clump of Spanish Moss on top of it before she sat near the edge to reflect. She knew after this that the challenge of her vendetta upped significantly.

That night, after extensive meditation and breath work, Maya's dreams were filled with the same type of memories as the previous few nights. Scenes of the last time she saw certain people—her parents, Aunt Nekisha, and, more recently, Elijah, along with each of the group who lived in the woods. She was detached by day but conflicted by night. Her dream world was like a megaphone from her bones.

Three down, three to go.

10 This Thing Of Ours

A small restaurant in Mid-City was celebrating its 75th year. You went there for an old-world feel, including the music. You went there for Sicilian-style red gravy on the cannelloni and a carafe of the house Lambrusco. You went there as a New Orleans tradition. You definitely went there when the owner Anthony Rizzo beckoned you there.

Inside, past the tables in the front dining section, the bar with drawings posted of regulars' heads by the manager Ms. Donna, and a handful of employees dressed in black with red ties, you veered a step to the left for the private room, making sure to avoid any food runners dashing from the busy kitchen on the right.

That room was where Anthony Rizzo was holding court the same as his father before him. Like in the front, the yellow wall was filled with maps of Italy or Sicily, ads for brands no longer around, and various family photos. In the private room, though, the two black and white family photos were blown up in size.

One of them was set in Cefalu, a small coastal village to the east of Palermo, and the namesake of the restaurant. It was fitting, because the Italian part of the French Quarter was called Piccola Palermo, or Little Palermo, starting around the 1840s. This was back when Italian gangs were named after the city they'd left, before the Matranga's became the first Mafia crime family in the U.S. by pulling together the disorganization a bit, which was further tightened up by a 24-year-old rising in their ranks who took over things when they decided to retire a few decades later.

His name was Dominick Rizzo, the father of current crime boss Anthony Rizzo, and he was the man who firmly shaped the Black Hand gangs into what we know as La Cosa Nostra or the Mafia. Truth be told, the New Orleans version was the most similar to the Sicilian model in a strong way, unlike that of the East Coast that came decades later. Although Crescent City leadership structure was in place, there were plenty of familiar affiliates and peripheral members. That allowed the web of the Mafia to more deeply permeate the entire city.

"Tony," said Nick Noto, speaking with his eyes as much as his mouth.

Anthony Rizzo raised an index finger while he finished chewing his steak, before jabbing at his mouth with a white linen napkin.

"Nicky, come on," he said. "What do you want from me? The way I look at it, your job got easier. Don't have to worry no more about Joey Lyons zipping his lip. Make sure his widow gets something nice. With my regards."

"He had a big fuckin' mouth too," echoed capo Nofio Morici while he poured himself more wine.

Louis Rizzo Sr. had been studying his brother.

"We had nothin' to do with this?"

"What are you saying to me, Lou?"

"Hmm," added Morici.

Louis raised his whole hand. Not one finger but five of them pointed at Morici.

"That's enough outta you. Shut it."

Morici smirked, "Who me?" and sipped his vino.

Louis muttered, "Who? Who? You a fuckin' owl?" before continuing, "Tony, I'm makin' sure our hands are clean."

Anthony shook his head. "Feels like you're talking for Lou Jr. His boy got hit. I understand the pain. Must be bottled up in him real bad. But Lou, nobody's keeping you out of the loop."

Morici nodded a little too vigorously.

"Listen, jerk-off. Get enough respect to know better. Watch yourself," said Louis.

"Why I gotta be a jerk-off?" protested Morici.

"If the shoe fits," said Louis with frozen contempt. "Prefer I call you a fuck-up?"

"Whoa, whoa. Lou, Lou," the other two said, to which Louis responded, "My bad."

Noto tried again. "Tony, how long have we known each other?"

"Back since you were mayor of Kenner. The 80s."

"I've had you and your family in my home many times. You've been gracious enough to extend the same to me and Elena. Your fishing camp in Grand Isle was my second home in the 90s."

"It was," said Anthony.

"Grazie for that, Tony. I mean it. You would also say—correct me if I'm wrong—that I've always advised you from my mind and my heart in a way that's only benefited you."

"You have, Nicky. That's all correct."

"You can understand why I want you to share my heightened concern. Everything this week doesn't feel random. It's escalating. I'm concerned our cartel partners are wanting to take over things."

Anthony gestured for Morici to pour him another glass of Lambrusco from the now quarter-full carafe. He took a sip before he spoke.

"Gentlemen, look around us. A private room. The best restaurant in town, in my opinion. Food from the homeland. Sal runs it real good for me. This wine—what more do I need to drink? Lou, Nofio, Nicky. This is the good life. The steak, the arancini, the vino. I've had governors, mayors, judges, senators, congressmen, even a vice president of this very country right here at the table. They came to show due respect and to receive it."

Anthony raised his right hand and circled it around his head.

"I'm talking about the big birds that fly up above everyone else. Not big bird. None of that Sesame Street shit."

"Nah," said Morici.

Anthony continued, "I too consider myself a big bird flying up high. Living the good life that I've worked for. Decades. I can't be concerned with what flies do. It's not serious business to me. Not everything goes my way. Or your way, your way, your way," he said pointing at each man.

"Never has," agreed Morici while Louis eyeballed him disparagingly.

"That teaches us patience, tenacity, like knocking at a door until they answer, so while I agree that it hasn't been a great week, I cannot and will not be convinced it's any more than some flies. Flies that get swatted with a cheap little plastic doohickey, not hammered with a baseball bat.

Am I making myself clear?"

"Yes, Tony," said Noto while Louis nodded with a "Yeah" and Morici unsurprisingly said, "Always been clear."

"Good," said Anthony. "Mangia, bevi, e sii felice. Eat, drink, and be merry, to anyone who no longer knows the old tongue."

Louis gestured at Morici who eyeballed him and slowly muttered, "Sono Siciliano," as he cut his steak.

While Anthony and Louis repeated it and sliced theirs too, they missed Noto biting his lip. It felt like a time of reckoning to him and it'd only been a week. A week that included rats all over Cefalu, including on this very table. If he were to be so bold as to tell Anthony Rizzo, of all people, that his power and money were blinders to a real threat, then it wouldn't be with others around.

"I don't feel good about this. Tony, decades ago you started hungry but now you're talking full. The Mexican and Chinese drug cartels are ruthless. Not flies at all," Noto only said to himself then continued with his food too.

In his way, Anthony said "C'mere" and curled an index finger at Noto who was only two feet away. That meant you come to me, not I come to you. As per usual, once Noto leaned in, Anthony firmly gripped the other man's right forearm while speaking.

"Black punk who thinks he's gonna bring down Leon Mancuso. Let's talk about it tomorrow," said Anthony discreetly to Noto. "That's something I'm concerned about."

While most of the table enjoyed the rest of their lunch,

Theresa and Cecilia Rizzo, Louis' wife and daughter, were shopping at Lakeside Mall. Cecilia was a theatre student at NOCCA, the premiere New Orleans arts high school, to the consternation of her father. Theresa caused his blood pressure to jump too, so she'd learned years ago to run up credit cards at her numerous mall visits when he wasn't home to see her enter with shopping bags galore.

Louis Jr. was taking a break from his rounds of checking in and handling a few pickups at various Rizzo businesses. Most of them had such a circuitous chain of title that Maya and her group, much less the general public, had no idea the massive number of for-profit or for-money laundering businesses they truly had.

For now, the son of the underboss was visiting one of his girlfriends at the corner of Buick and Pocahontas. No way his parents could know about her. They saw him marrying an Italian girl who went to Sacred Heart or even Ursuline Academy, not an ebony girl from Gentilly.

Theresa was the first home, followed by Jr., who'd picked up his sister Cecilia at the end of school, and lastly by Sr. right after sunset, which came early in December. Christmas decor draped the outside of their house and a large fir tree inside was filled underneath with gifts.

An hour later, all were at the dining room table but Sr., who entered as Cecilia was saying, "I performed my monologue today. Ms. Tanner said I showed strength, vulnerability, and curiosity."

"A monologue, huh," said her father who walked past the family's grandfather clock before seeing his plate at the table compared to everyone else's. "Theresa," he grumbled and pointed to the compare-and-contrast.

"Mono means one, so it's me solo. No other..." Cecilia said before she was cut off.

"Mono means one," mocked her older brother. "Then why don't they call it a duologue if it's two people?"

Cecilia fired back. "Mono's also what you get every month from kissing hoes."

"Cecilia, language!" chided her mother, who then looked at Louis Jr., shook her head, and responded to her husband, "Lou, you know what the doctor said."

"You guys get seafood manicotti and I get stuck with rabbit food," as he looked down with disdain.

"Happy Easter, dad," laughed Jr.

The older man roughly grabbed his son's plate and switched it with his own.

"Okay, Mr. Funny. How you feel now?"

"I ain't eatin' this."

Before his father could respond, everything went dark. The sun had gone down hours before and all they could see out the window was that the neighbors' lights remained on.

"Lou, go outside and check the power box," said Sr. "Grab a flashlight."

"Dad, I got a light on my phone," said the younger man while he begrudgingly got up. Passed through the doorway, slipped on shoes, and stepped outside.

When he turned along the side of the house where multiple lines fed into a standard electrical box, his head was met with sudden impact. Everything went black and he fell upon the grass.

For the last three years, Maya had been growing bamboo in the woods near her house. Once it matured after the first year of growth, Zachary chopped down a couple tall stalks. As instructed, he cut sixteen pieces at 3-foot length with around 1 ½-inch circumference.

The group used these bamboo sticks, two for each, as fighting sticks for Kali or Eskrima, depending on who you asked. Maya had learned this Filipino style from Sifu Julius Mosley, and it was effective for up-close fighting. The sticks were ideal for striking each other to get comfortable with pain. Arms, legs, stomach, and shoulders were the recipients of this.

It was one of those same bamboo sticks that had delivered a sharp blow to Jr's head, knocking him out immediately. Maya zip-tied each wrist to a corresponding ankle to keep him neutralized.

"That's what I thought," she said softly. Her assumption was that they'd send out the son to check the box after she flipped the main breaker switch. His tell-tale sign was cologne that had been vigorously sprayed to cover up certain smells.

When the front door opened shortly after, still to a dark home, the rest of the family sitting at the table groaned.

"Nothing, Lou?" asked Theresa. "Lou?"

Instead, an unfamiliar voice pierced through the darkness as its source moved closer to them.

"I'm here for Big Lou."

Louis Sr.'s thundering reply of, "Who the fuck you think you are?" drowned out Theresa's "Oh, my God" and Cecilia's shuddering. Rizzo's throwing of his, or rather Jr's, plate missed Maya, and crashed against the grandfather clock. The ricotta cheese helped some of the manicotti shells stick firmly against the clock.

"Girls, out!" he said to his wife and daughter who grabbed hands and helped each other away from the unfolding scene.

Louis Sr. got to his feet. "You come in my house, better be ready to die," he announced to where he last heard the voice.

From his other side, he was struck hard upon the chest with one stick and to his crotch with another, before Maya disappeared back into the darkness.

"Fuck!" He grimaced in pain as he reached down to where it radiated in dual spots.

Two more parallel swings from the back crashed against his hamstrings.

"You motherfucker!" while he grabbed anything he could reach on the table and flung it behind him.

Maya had already quickly moved to his left side. This time she made impact to his shoulder and big gut. When he called out, "Ummmmph!" she kept swinging. He reached out with his hands in the dark, only to have his left wrist and right knuckles crunched by the bamboo sticks.

Louis Sr. stepped back. He needed to get to the nearby cabinet.

"Alright, alright. What do you want?"

For the second time, the unfamiliar voice cut through.

"This is a long time coming. Your family's run this city for decades. That's the reason things don't get any better. One reason anyway. You keep stacking up money while people are leaving. Hospitality industry jobs don't pay anything. You get mayors and whoever else to do your bidding. Bleed the public money dry. Schools stay broke. All the violence. Your name's on that," she said.

"God almighty. Get off your damn high horse. Everybody's tryin' to get over in New Orleans," he responded. Maya could hear that he was moving while he said, "I'm a businessman. You think what I do is any different from some Joe Schmo CEO?"

"You're the shadow government and..."

"Hold on! Hold on! Money means influence. Everywhere."

"You exploit people."

"Psssh. My give-a-damn is long since busted. Who doesn't look out for their own self-interest? It's business," while still slowly moving.

"When the Rizzo crime family's taken down, I know it won't make a difference. Not much of one anyway. Don't care. You had my parents killed. You're paying for it. This is my vendetta."

"Vendetta?" he sneered as the lights came back to life. Now he could clearly see who was standing a few feet beyond a human's length away as he rushed over to the cabinet. Cecilia had slipped out the back door, flipped the breaker on, and eliminated Maya's darkness advantage. Louis Sr. immediately trained his gun on her, which she didn't know he had until hearing, "Now look who has the upper hand. Before I put a bullet in your head, who the fuck are you?"

"Who am I? You don't remember Joey Lyons' big party three years ago? Everything that came from that?"

"You? That was you? You're that Black chick," he realized.

"First time one of you hasn't called me a bitch."

He laughed, still in pain. "That makes you feel good?" As he stepped closer. Gun trained on her. "I'm bitch shooting bitch you bitch down bitch like bitch the bitch you bitch are bitch. How 'bout that?"

Maya was glad he'd come closer. Always better to be tight in with an opponent holding a gun. She had a bamboo stick in both her left and right hands. Both cocked in chamber position behind each shoulder.

The left, flung at the gun itself, was a decoy to get him to fire the gun or potentially even knock it out of his clasp. He was struck by it directly across his gun hand, fired at the ceiling, cried out in pain, and that was all the time Maya needed. She was the one dominant and deadly.

She'd already been moving around the table when the lights were off to familiarize herself with the room. Knew there was about 5-foot width between the table and the wall. Gauged from his voice that he was 6-feet away before he stopped moving. That was a ninja activity they practiced in the woods. Voice and distance apart.

Manicotti stayed stuck against the grandfather clock while it chimed 7:00PM.

Maya started with her left foot, followed by a quick right. As she was about to make the next and final left step forward, she shifted her core to the right. When her foot hit the ground, her body torqued from right to left, and her right arm swung just after the step. Her weapon traveled as swift and strong as any metal sword.

The bamboo stick found Louis Rizzo Sr's head with so much impact it caused more bodily trauma than he had experienced on any level, including when he survived getting shot to the head as a 17-year-old in the parking lot of Club Cinderella on Old Gentilly Rd run by the biggest loan shark in town. That place was now vacant, next to a snoball spot, and ironically not far from the modest little neighborhood that bizarrely had streets of Native American names intersecting with early 1900s car names, including where Lou Jr. spent time.

He tried to fire another desperation shot, but she batted the gun out of his hand before striking him ferociously in the head twice more to make sure he was handled. If he'd been unlucky, he'd have stayed alive with brain damage and internal bleeding. Maya's grace was the final two strikes to make sure he wasn't getting up.

She placed the Spanish Moss on Rizzo, paused a moment to meditate, then left.

11 The Beyond

Multiple Jefferson Parish law enforcement officials were on the scene while Louis Jr. furiously paced and clenched his hands. A shocked Cecilia sat with blank eyes, and Theresa performed accordingly.

Theresa had known for years that Lou had women on the side. Tolerated it. Ignored it. Focused on her kids. Their arguments had increased so much that it'd been the harsh baseline of their relationship for years. Part of her was glad he was gone, but she definitely didn't want him going out like this.

"A woman hit man? A hit woman?" She thought while asking anyone within earshot, "Is this voodoo?" about the Spanish moss in the evidence bag on the table.

Cecilia was the only one, beyond the late Louis Sr., who had actually seen Maya. After flipping on the main breaker switch, she went to her brother to help him, and saw Maya leave their house. Cecilia thought they'd exchanged glances, but though she expected to be the next target, the woman in the cowl simply left. Maya hadn't seen her, of course, only detected movement to her left.

"Don't say a thing to anybody but Uncle Tony. Okay?" her mother had made clear along with keeping in close when Cecilia was being interviewed by the police about her experience with what had happened.

When, at last, law enforcement left and media outside gave up on interviewing any of the Rizzo's, at least for the day, Theresa called Anthony Rizzo. Within less than half an hour, both his driver and Nick Noto pulled up separately in the driveway.

"I've got news for you, Tony," Noto said discreetly.

"Save it, Nicky. This is family. My brother. They got Lou. Fucking got him."

"You'll want to know this," insistently.

Anthony reached out with his right hand, clasped Noto's forearm tightly, and pulled the other man slightly toward him, before saying, "Not now. Zip it."

He shook a ringed index finger.

"On my name, this will be avenged."

Anthony greeted Theresa with a hug and, "Marcella will be over later with some food. Che merde de giornata."

"Si, what a shitty day," she agreed.

"I'll take care of this. We'll find him. Nobody does this to Lou."

While Noto looked on, Theresa made a peripheral glance to make sure Cecilia was in the other room before saying, "Tony, it wasn't a him. A woman killed my Lou. You can't let nobody know that. Or the voodoo stuff. She put Spanish Moss on him."

Anthony was shocked. "A woman?"

"Cecilia saw her. Black girl. Had her hood up but yeah. She thought around 25 to 30-years old, but you can't tell with the Blacks. Cecilia snuck outside to turn the power back on. That's how the killer came after Lou in the dark."

Anthony sighed. "My brother. A woman?"

Noto inhaled a full belly of air through his nostrils. He needed to talk with Rizzo, but first he announced, "I'm going to step outside and make a phone call."

"You sure?" asked Anthony, looking oddly at Noto.

"I'll explain when I come back."

Noto stood in the driveway, looked for a text from "EB," and called the number. He used a code with each initial one letter away for security's sake. That meant he was actually calling "FC."

"Hey, Mr. Nick."

"Frankie. I'm here at Lou Rizzo's. Somebody hit him. Don't spread that around."

"Oh, maaaaan. Thee Lou Rizzo? Sorry to hear that."

"Yeah. Remember what you were starting to tell me earlier about what happened a few days ago? Will you continue?"

Nick Noto had deep connections. Many on a high level who he could reach out to for a favor or for information. In some instances, he needed things handled on a street level. That's what Frankie Calimari was for.

"I broke into that lawyer's office. Jason Polidore. The one goin' against Judge Mancuso."

"Frankie, I know all that. Skip ahead," said an annoyed Noto.

"Alright. I saw in his files who's fundin' it. He had a name on his notepad. You know that WWL investigative reporter?"

"Frankie. That I also know. You already told me. Jump ahead to the secretary."

"Got it. I was lookin' through his stuff. Secretary shows up. After hours, but I guess she left somethin' behind. Dunno if she heard me first or I heard her. Didn't want to shoot no female, Mr. Nick. Had my piece out, though, to scare her. She stared at me, sayin', 'I knew it. I knew it. I knew it.' Told her to shut up."

"I already know this part."

"I'm just tellin' you she said it three times."

"And," coaxed Noto.

I asked her, "What do you know, baby?" She said, 'When my boss decided he was callin' out Judge Mancuso, I knew the judge's friends would show up, especially after Jason turned down that $50,000 to drop out."

"Frankie, you're killing me. I already heard it. All this abstract fumbling. What about the fighter?"

"The secretary—her name was Raven—she said she was worth more to me alive. She knew what was gonna happen. Saw my face. Told me, 'I can be a good friend to you. Your mole on the inside. But you gonna pay me. I bet you didn't know Maya Gaines is still in New Orleans. That martial arts fighter."

"Right there. That's where you stopped. Continue from this point. What about Maya?"

"Raven said, 'That blind bitch never went away. Her...'"

"Wait, wait, wait," said Noto. "Blind? Can't be."

"That's what she said."

Nick Noto's mind was reeling. Spanish Moss connected Lou Rizzo's death to Joey Lyons, T-Boy, and Flora Mosley. How does a blind woman do all this? He also realized something else. Anthony Rizzo was in grave danger.

But first, "Keep going."

"She said, 'That blind bitch never went away. Her hideout's in New Orleans. Way down at the end.' That's what Raven said."

"Did you get the..."

Frankie cut off Noto. "Already goin' there, Mr. Nick. That Raven is a smart one. She told me if I paid her monthly, starting with good faith money right then, she'd tell me the address and all the Polidore updates. I said, 'What's to stop me from paying you, getting the address, and killing you after?' She said, 'You and me both on camera. Part of my job is to monitor the cameras after hours. You must've broken in when I was on the way here. Say you kill me. They got it all on video and you can't delete it.' She was thinkin'."

"Smart girl."

"Yeah, real smart. She said Maya got a straw house and it's..."

"Whoa, Frankie. A straw house?"

"Yeah."

"Like the Three Little Pigs? What specifically did she say?"

"Polidore helped Maya. She gave him the cash. He bought a lot and got a construction loan in his name to build the straw house."

"Frankie, a straw buyer is when...forget it. Tell me this. Do you have Maya's address?"

"I thought you'd never ask."

When Noto went back inside, Anthony Rizzo was sitting on the couch with Theresa and Cecilia. Louis Jr. met him at the door.

"I'm so sorry, Lou," while he gave him a hug.

"I'ma kill her. With a baseball bat. Fuck her up like she did to dad."

"Lou, Lou, Lou," Noto eased. "This will be handled.

Trust and believe that. Let me talk to your uncle first.”

After Noto pulled Anthony into his brother’s office for privacy, the crime boss said his piece.

“Nicky, we have a grieving family out there. This rudeness of yours is bothering me.”

“Tony, you’ll hear in a moment what’s been going on.”

Anthony sighed, “Look, give the coroner’s office a call. Y’know what, why don’t you just go to Harvey and talk to ‘em directly. We also need 2 barrels of whiskey.”

“Thirsty, Tony?”

“Something like that. Lou’s request. He told me, ‘Tony, if it so happens that I leave this earth before you, then I only want two things. One, take me out on the lake one last time. Two, no formaldehyde. Make sure the funeral house knows that. Lake Lawn.”

“Noto nodded. “By Metairie Cemetery. Right. Why no formaldehyde?”

Anthony’s eyes narrowed. “It’s gonna be the same for me whenever God says time’s up. Lou’s and my bisnonno, Pascal, our great grandfather, died on the boat here from Sicily. 1911. Our biznonna Giuseppa was said to have a way with words that made people do what she wanted. When they were about to throw bisnonno’s body overboard, she convinced the sailors to preserve him in whiskey. Guess they didn’t wanna mess with a pregnant woman”

“Ah, I see.”

“It’s Rizzo male family tradition at this point. That and the best Lambrusco recipe.”

Noto acknowledged it all but cautioned, “Got it,

Tony, but look. You need to go into hiding. Same person who got Lou most likely did Joey Lyons and the other two this week. That's why I was on the phone."

"You gonna say a woman serial killer too? Who's ever heard of that? Plus, what's it look like if I'm running scared?"

"Listen to me. There's a good chance the killer is that Black chick who was fighting in the warehouse for Joey. Remember the one that was at his place for the party? That whole mess three years ago?"

"You're saying she's returned?"

"I'm saying she never went away. Been in New Orleans the whole time. From what's been going down all week, it feels like she's been preparing for payback."

"You know what you're saying? Vendetta? I'm Anthony Fucking Rizzo."

"You definitely are," Noto agreed. "But don't forget. Her parents got taken out shortly after all that from the party hit the news. Both were in Federal pens. Plus, Joey had his guys firebomb the girl's house, but her aunt was the only body found. Think about it. She's getting revenge on everyone who messed with her family."

"You telling me a Black broad still wet behind the ears hit my brother and three other people?"

"It's crazier than that," said Noto. "She's blind. Must have happened when she was hiding out."

Anthony put his hands together, fingers up, as if to pray. He roughly ran them along his nose, in between his eyebrows, and to the top of his furrowed forehead.

"Do I need to clean out my ears? You said blind?"

"I did."

Anthony pursed his lips before saying, "I'm supposed to believe a blind Black broad is making us look like clowns. Theresa told me Lou Jr. didn't do anything because the chick knocked him out before she went inside. Did all that without seeing him and then my brother?"

"It gets better. She's working with that lawyer Jason Polidore who's trying to bring down Leon."

"The silver lining. Then I'm gonna make sure they both got something coming. You got her address?"

Noto shook his head up and down.

Anthony huffed, "I'm not going into hiding. It's not even in question. She wants a vendetta? Against the Rizzo's?"

He began to tap the table hard with his finger.

"Blind. Got to be kidding me. It stops now. What's her name?"

"Maya," Noto said. "Maya Gaines."

"Maya Gaines, who the fuck are you?" Anthony asked to the ceiling. "I'll have Nofio put a team together now. Go to her place. Take care of this."

He gestured to the door. "Look what she did to the family. Lou's leaving a widow, Cecilia, Lou Jr. Speaking of Lou Jr., he's not gonna be one of Nofio's soldiers. So ready to explode he'll end up shooting our own guys."

Anthony slowly clapped four times before speaking again to the ceiling.

"You don't know what I got for you, Maya. Whoever you think you are, your luck's over. I got garlic bullets for you."

It wasn't an hour later when Nofio Morici and a crew of five soldiers crossed the Mississippi River in a plain white van. Not long after, they crossed a second bridge.

"Remember, boss man wants her brought back alive. He wants to do the hit himself. For Lou. Get ready. She knows all kinda Bruce Lee shit too," said Morici, the Rizzo family capo.

"Fuck outta here. I got her ass handled," said a chiseled-jaw man called Foot.

They parked at the edge of the woods and all moved quietly through the trees. There was no driveway or path, so, as instructed, Foot led with a small flashlight pointed downward. Each man in turn was in a row behind him, left fingertips pressing on the back of the one in front of him, right hand clenching a pistol.

Soon enough, the light glowing from a house not far ahead was their beacon. Foot extinguished his flashlight and slowed as the masked men moved into formation side by side. They were ready to bring about a festival of fear.

When they reached the house, Foot and one of the others stood in front of the door. After Morici quietly counted down "3,2,1," while holding up the same number of fingers, the two men stepped forward together and kicked the door in.

By the time they reached the group of six, those living in the house had martial arts weapons in hand that were quickly dropped to the floor to follow orders in light of the guns trained on them.

Soon after, Morici and his soldiers led the group out of the house at gunpoint. Foot was pushing a young lady ahead of him who hadn't put up much of a protest. Hadn't tried a thing.

"What I tell you? She ain't so tough," Foot popped off.

12 The Confession

"Tony, come to bed. It's late. Getting cold," said Marcella, his wife of 48 years, eyeing the window where they could see an oak tree's branches shaking in the wind of the arriving arctic blast.

Anthony Rizzo, as feared as any man in New Orleans and for miles around, sat on the couch holding up two framed photos he'd taken off the mantle. He was surrounded by matchless luxury mixed with a modest homey feel.

"They made this photo before Lou and I went out to the gully to catch cowan. Look how we're smiling then. That's the before. We each got one. Lou didn't follow our daddy's instructions to a T. 'Hold that bag way out,' he told us. Lou didn't listen. Had his bag just hanging when we walked back. Bouncing against him. If that turtle didn't lock its jaw on Lou's leg through the burlap. Had him screaming bloody murder."

Marcella had heard this story several times before, but she wasn't going to remind him of that. Our life, our stories, and our memories are all we have. She knew he was missing his brother something fierce, so she put a hand on his shoulder.

"The kids are getting so old," she said, looking at the other photo with the two of them, the twins, and Little Tommy. They'd had kids late. The Feds messing with Anthony led to eight years behind bars just before his 40s.

"Speaking of the twins, I need to check in with them.

They called earlier, but I was on the phone."

Marcella knew well not to question calls at that time of the night. It's just how it was. Francesca, who they called Franny, was CEO of the top sanitation company in New Orleans. Well, not the top one, but the company who always got the contract. Using the low bid trick always worked.

Low bid had to be accepted but charge whatever once the ink dries on the contract. No one comes checking. Jacked up costs and time overruns were the New Orleans way.

Franny was at work.

Her twin sister Angela, who was known in the family as Rose, headed up the Rizzo's real estate management company. Whether it was in New Orleans or out in the rural parishes, their holdings were extensive. Rose was also at work.

Thomas, or Tommy, on the other hand was doing the Bourbon Street thing. Upstairs in the office of one of their strip clubs. Pants at his ankles, while the new dancer did a line of coke off his manhood. He was the baby brother who got grief for not wanting to grow up.

On this particular night, though, he would quickly age 5-10 years.

"Daddy, are you serious?" asked Francesca.

"I'm sorry to say I am."

"Uncle Lou. Wow. Why don't I come on over?"

"No, no, Franny," said Anthony. "I appreciate it, but I won't be up much longer anyway."

"Alright."

"I was also calling to ask about Finley."

"Sure, what's up?" She wondered what he'd done this time. The owner of Trio Trash, named as such because he was Finley Santos III, was a rich kid with family connections who loved island vacations, New Orleans parties, and to stay in the public eye.

Keeping Trio Trash going wasn't even in his top five, so that's where Francesca came in. Plus, the right people knew she was Tony Rizzo's daughter. Not only did they mind their manners with her, but she made it clear she was about her business. Though she'd occasionally hit the town with Craig Forstall, Francesca Rizzo was married to her work.

"He loves the camera too much," said Anthony. "Used to be photos of guys like us only when the Feds spied on a meeting or we're walking into a courthouse."

"I know, daddy. Fin wants to be a man of the people."

"What he wants to be is the next Diamond Jim," huffed her father.

"Who's that?"

"Back in the day, Diamond Jim was a made man with a bunch of restaurants. Liked to hang out with celebrities. Dressed all fancy. Diamonds on his teeth. On his clothes too. Alla that. Changed his name to Moran, but he was a Brocato.

Francesca was astonished. "A Sicilian?"

"I know," he agreed. "Too flashy. Complete opposite of keeping a low profile. There's a reason I've had longevity, Franny. These photo ops I see. Does Finley drive around looking for fucking cameras?"

"It's his way, daddy. Plus, everyone has a phone."

"Stupid ass doesn't realize nobody was going to his

restaurants. That's why we had Robert Beaty take over them all. Call it Black-owned. It's a gimmick, but it works. He's charging more on that menu than at the white places. That Black bastard's on fire."

"Rob's definitely got it going," said Francesca. "I think Fin feels like if he's out there publicly, it helps him look more legit."

"Nah, he's a people pleaser. Not enough to have bookoo money. He wants to be beloved too. Like Diamond Jim. The only thing people love is what you can do for them."

She laughed. "You sound cynical."

He returned her laugh. "They say wisdom has a cynical bias. So, tell me. Jefferson Parish renewed the contract or that new Councilman still grandstanding?"

She paused. "We're not quite there."

"Hmm. He'll be playing ball by Friday."

"Okay, daddy." She took a deep breath. "The thing with Uncle Lou. You have any reason to be concerned? For yourself."

"That'll be the day," he scoffed. "Last time somebody came for me it was a snot nosed punk name of Robbie Corolla. 5th grade. I cleaned his clock too."

"I bet you did. Tell mom I'll come by after work to help cook for Aunt Theresa."

"Ti amo, figlia mia."

"Love you too, daddy."

Before Anthony could call Rose, a familiar number rang him. It was Nofio Morici.

"Boss man, I got her. Didn't put up a fight either."

He looked across the warehouse at the six people

bound and seated on the floor. One of them whispered to the Black woman in her 20s.

"I can't believe they think you're Maya."

"Ssssh, Lil Bit," said Ayana through her teeth.

"Good work, Nofio."

"I'm not a jerk off after all, huh?"

"You still harping on that? Lou's body's still warm. Keep the girl alive. I'll come by after some sleep. Which warehouse?"

"Harvey by Boomtown Casino."

"I appreciate you. Give your men my thanks."

Anthony heard a noise in the kitchen. Normally he wouldn't have thought a thing of it, but after Lou got hit he was a little concerned.

"Marce, that you?" he called out.

No answer.

"Marce?"

He grabbed his drinking glass from the coffee table and went to the kitchen to see...

"Gatta, what you doing?" as his cat played with a stray piece of paper. He laughed and thought of his brother's upcoming funeral. It would be on time the way his brother preferred. Short and sweet. Half hour tops. "My Way" by Sinatra while his open casket was brought in and something sad but triumphant by Andrea Bocelli when the pall bearers walked him to the hearse. Gotta have somebody talking about Lou throwing out the first pitch at a Zephyr's game. Despite everything else, that remained one of his proudest moments

Anthony put his glass in the sink and returned to the living room.

Standing where he had been sitting a figure had appeared. She was holding nunchucks in ready position over her right shoulder. His gun was in the garage, which may as well have been a continent away. He had bullets out there soaking in garlic oil. Time had mostly discounted the efficacy of this technique, but Mafia tradition had it that the person shot would suffer more and be less likely to heal.

Anthony couldn't help but gasp.

"How'd you get away?"

"What?"

"You gotta be Maya. They got the wrong one."

"Wait, what do you...?"

Anthony shook his head in said in disgust, "They got the wrong Black broad."

Maya realized immediately what he meant. It hit hard. Rizzo's people had found the house in the woods, and they got Ayana. Probably the others too. All but Zachary.

Anthony realized he needed to keep his mouth shut. Noto said she was blind. If that was really true, he didn't want to telegraph his moves.

He was over 10-feet away from her. Couch between them. "Here's how I find out," he thought. Reached down and took off both his slippers before creeping around the room as quietly as he could to her right.

Anthony threw one of the slippers right back to where he'd been. Saw her respond to it, and she inched forward in that direction.

"You know why I'm here, right?" she said.

This time he didn't speak. Instead, he threw the second slipper a few feet in front of her. Once he did, two things happened quickly.

Anthony had been eyeballing the buck head with imposing antlers mounted on the wall. It's why he moved in that direction in the first place. He wasn't young, but he still had fight in him while he ran as quickly as he could. Grabbed the prize from the wall, briefly recalled his shot back in 2003 at the hunting camp between Ama and Avondale, and headed toward Maya.

For her part, Maya took a left step and fired the nunchucks to where she expected a 5'9" man's head would be. The wood met nothing but air. She figured he must have moved back quickly, so as she stepped forward with her right foot, she swung the nunchucks backhand from left to right. She heard him behind her too late.

All of this—Anthony's and Maya's movements—happened in a few seconds. The culmination of it all was him shoving the buck's antlers into her back. His momentum and her own steps forward had them both falling to the ground.

The noise of a taxidermy buck crashing to the floor elicited a call from upstairs.

"Tony! Tony! You alright?!"

"Bring a gun!" he yelled, striking Maya as hard as he could with both fists.

Two things had registered with Maya. Not only did the Rizzo's now know her home base for the past three years, but he must have found out she was blind.

"It's not possible," she thought. "No way Polidore would give her up like that. Maybe Rizzo's guys got it out of the kids."

Maya was on the ground, and Anthony was on his

knees, but she was far more agile than the man who had 45+ years on her. She blocked his punches as best she could by holding the nunchucks horizontally a foot in front of her face with both hands.

Using a method learned from Sifu Mosley, she timed his strikes, and when Maya anticipated the next ones, she rolled sharply to her right, pulling herself out from under him, moved behind, swung the nunchucks across the front of his head, and caught it with her left.

Maya then pulled back roughly, choking him with the seven links of chain against the fleshy part of his neck just above the Adam's apple cartilage. He jerked forward and rocked back to shake her loose, but Maya braced herself and didn't give up the grip.

"Krrrrrrg," he gurgled out.

Just then, a gunshot blasted past Maya's head into the wall. Marcella was shouting from the stairs.

Maya ducked down behind Anthony while he gestured no to his wife with flailing hands.

"You try and shoot me, you're gonna hit him!" said Maya as she let up a bit on the chain's tightness against Anthony's neck. He could speak after coughing and gasping for air.

"Marce, no," he cautioned.

"But Tony," she gestured. "You want me to call...?"

"Omerta!" he shouted angrily. "Don't call nobody."

"I meant Nofio or one of the guys."

Anthony closed his eyes. "No, they're way down on the West Bank."

Maya registered this piece of information. All of it must have happened after Louis Rizzo's death. She and

Zachary had gone up to the lake to walk and sit for a while and hadn't been home yet.

She spoke to Anthony, "Usually when something bad happens, people think why me? But you, I bet you never wonder."

"Yadda, yadda, yadda. That's a matter of opinion," he shot back. "You have no idea how many businesses got their startup money from me. All the good I've done."

"Oh, really? So many people would love to be in my shoes," Maya responded.

"Shut your stupid trap. You're no different than me. My people started this whole thing to protect our own. Same thing you're doing. Irish didn't do it. French, Spanish, none of them had heart. You Blacks couldn't do it. Only my people."

"Mafia might've started out for the right reasons," she said, "but look what it turned into."

"Psssh," he retorted. "Look what you turned into. Now you got blood on your hands. It's a slippery slope. Keep thinking you're better or different than me and see what happens. You're too young to know, but when the Feds shook things up in the early 90s, guess what happened?"

Anthony paused.

"That's a fucking question."

"I don't know."

"What's that? I can't hear you?"

Maya said steadily, "I said, 'I don't know.' But I know you're gonna tell me all about it."

"Better believe it," he said haughtily. "Ask anybody how bad the 90s were in New Orleans. It was the wild west. Reason why is my people got taken off the board for a bit. Without us holding things together, the city turned savage. People getting shot left and right. Every man for himself. New Orleans needs us.”

He didn’t go deep enough to tell her he hadn’t been running things for even a decade when the Feds got him too in the early 90s. Didn’t breath a word that the whole reason he’d been put in place barely after turning 30 was because his father had a fatal heart attack at the 1984 World’s Fair. The two of them were in a gondola car crossing 320-feet above the Mississippi River when it happened. It was Anthony’s urging that got Mob Boss Dominick Rizzo on the rinky dink ride. He’d never told anyone that this decision killed his father at age 73. Now he himself was about to die at the exact same age.

She shook her head. “You have people thinking that. You might even believe it. The city’s in bad shape now, but you don’t care as long as you get that tourist money and everything else. Who can take the blame more than you? Who’s been running the city and state for as long as you? You’re the one who makes sure no one who’ll change things is elected. We only get new names with familiar skeletons”

He scoffed. “Mafia kingpin Anthony Rizzo. That’s all you think you see. I’m Sicilian, but I’m also a proud American. And I make things happen. I don’t do anything different from the people who they say built this country and the ones on top right now up in Washington. You take me out and nothing changes in New Orleans either. Know what happens in a beehive if the queen bee dies? They raise a new one. The bees keep being bees. That’s New Orleans too. Business keeps on. Being what it is.”

"That may be so," said Maya. "I know corruption is way too entrenched here for me to change much of anything. All you've done to keep people who look like me poor and uneducated. As long as you profit, right. But I'm here for one reason."

"Who are you?" Marcella called out.

"My name is vendetta," replied Maya before continuing with Anthony, "You gotta pay for my parents and my aunt. Franklin and Eugenia wouldn't have been locked up in a Federal pen if you didn't force him to do a pill mill from his pharmacy. Then everything with the club."

"Sounds like a bunch of mumbo jumbo," muttered Marcella.

"That was your father? Franklin Gaines. I wondered why 'Gaines' sounded so familiar. I had garlic bullets ready for what you did to my brother," said Anthony before he took a deep breath of realization that his life was about to end.

"Now you know why I'm here," as she again tightened the chain against Anthony's neck and pulled back. He began gurgling again and fought back to no avail.

Maya stared at Marcella. "This is the time to pray if you want. While he's still alive."

Marcella dropped the gun to her side. While her husband was being choked out and breathing his last breath, she cried, and shook, and said, "L'eterno riposo donagli, o Signore. Splenda a lui la luce perpetua. Riposi in pace." Sounded like a bitter symphony. She got through it twice before saying, "Amen," so distraught she couldn't pick up the gun without her hands shaking too much.

As before, Maya placed a small batch of Spanish Moss on his chest. Like she had seen her mother do, Maya meditated and did breathwork while Marcella Rizzo yelled and screamed in anguish. A bumpy empire was over. Or was it?

13 Ghosts & Fear

A RARE EXTREME COLD FRONT HAD FULLY MOVED INTO THE New Orleans area by daylight on Thursday. Meteorologists, weathercasters, and everyone else were stunned that snow was expected for Friday. The city might have minor flurries every few years, but the snow would always melt by the time it reached the ground. This was far different.

Vinh Nguyen peered out a window of his house on stilts.

"You must be kidding. I'm in the middle of nowhere, but you're telling me the Rizzo's couldn't take care of a fuckity fuck blind girl. Now I have to be careful?"

On the other end of the call, Nick Noto pursed his lips. He was used to difficult clients. That's what he did.

"Vinh," he said. "Maya told Tony's wife this is all about vendetta for her parents and her aunt. She's knocked off Flora Mosley, T-Boy, Joey Lyons, Louis Rizzo, and now Tony Rizzo. She's a giant killer. Yeah, you need to watch your back."

Nguyen started stretching his leg, which wound him up into full on Vinnie mode.

"Four people have my number," he started. "I'll tell you who. Two people who run my businesses, my real estate agent, and you. None of you know where I'm at. Only a phone number. I trust the others. Anthony Rizzo himself told me you could be trusted."

"Of course. And frankly, I'm filling in as head for now."

"If you are all trustworthy and only have a phone number anyway, then why would I worry about a stupid little bitch finding me? I don't like it here. No action. Me and this place are like cats and dogs, gators and goats, ponies and pigs. But if I'm hiding out here…"

He began to thunder, "I thought the Rizzo's could handle this. All the talk—'Vinh, we'll be great business partners.' 'Vinh, we have more muscle behind us than anyone around.' 'Vinh, our connections will be your connections.' Useless! My condolences to the Rizzo family. Get that straight, but why am I in a place with one road, where not even 1,000 people live, and you tell me to watch my back? It's so small here all I can see is my fuckity fuck back."

"I understand, Vinh. Keeping you in the loop. That's all."

Nguyen shook his head and pounded the wall with his open palms. Lisa, who handled his property management, mostly in the far stretch of New Orleans East called Versailles or Village L'est, had gotten him a great deal on the house in a very different area. In an ironic way, he loved that the little town, village, or unincorporated community was called Empire.

"I'm the king of nothing. Emperor of Empire," Nguyen groused.

Truth be told, Nguyen was feeling stir crazy. The years since escaping from the Terre Haute Federal Correctional Institute were taking a toll on him. Who knows where Dom Pecora, his fellow escapee, went? Nguyen pictured him in a much better place, with sexy women, men to do his bidding, and able to use his real name.

"Huy Tran. I am sick and tired of the name and the person known as Huy Tran," he said. Using the Vietnamese version of John Smith and peddling his story about a quiet life of retirement worked well. Very well. But Nguyen was missing the action. It wasn't an Empire by any definition. If he wanted to cut up a bit, he'd drive five minutes to Buras and hit Black Velvet for a drink. That had become as appealing as sipping sawdust.

He remembered when he first saw Maya subdue two robbers at the gas station on Elysian Fields, and when she came to his office at the back of the jewelry store to accept the push to be his bodyguard, though his real intent was to eventually make her his enforcer.

Nguyen recalled when she returned to his office and, in a cowardly way, declined the job before breaking his nose. Took out his guy Jimmy too. She did that while sighted, but now blind?

"Maya, Maya," he said. "You knock out a couple punks at the gas station and then fight in a warehouse under the Danziger Bridge to save your dear old dad. Now it's revenge time. We've both come a long way. Too bad you're not working for me. A blind assassin? We'd run New Orleans instead of the Rizzo's."

Local media plastered a version of the headline "Businessman Anthony Rizzo Dead At 73" atop their papers and posts, making sure only the PG obituary level details were included about this towering death. The unforgettable duality of his life was ignored, because it was largely unknown.

He was a man who financially seeded 100s of new white-owned businesses but also actively used his first bar to get underage Black kids hooked on drugs to up his profits. He was beloved and kind at the family dinner table but as ruthless on the streets as it got. A random Cefalu employee was quoted as calling him, "as sweet and kind as a bird flying through the forest," which had hundreds spitting out their coffee in surprise.

All of this despite his inclusion in various books on organized crime and far more truth talk in a range of news pieces published outside of New Orleans. A few national media sites even declared "Mafia boss Anthony Rizzo Killed."

By comparison, the death of his brother Louis elicited little media attention, but things were bustling behind the scenes. Nick Noto had stepped into the lead spot until new leadership was handled.

Nofio Morici wasn't about to be promoted. The narrative, fair or not, ever since the big boss's death was that it went down because Morici got the wrong person. Didn't matter that he followed orders.

It was getting to him.

"Hey, Monty. Keep your fuckin' eyes offa me," he said to one of the soldiers in the warehouse with him. It wasn't so much necessarily for Montana, named because he loved the movie *Scarface* and Tony Montana, but to send a message to all the men there.

"Don't play with me," because of being concerned that he himself might not make it out of the warehouse.

A query rang from across the big room. "Since you messed up, why don't you let us go?"

Morici stalked over to14-year old Elijah and said, "The hell you say to me?"

"Whatever I want," responded Elijah. "You all took off your masks. We can ID you. I'm speaking my mind. You not gonna kill us."

"Elijah," said the others, but he wouldn't be quiet.

"No. I was against this whole vendetta because I thought it'd be bad for Maya. But the worst part is this ho ass punk. Not only gets the wrong person but five more of us too."

At that, Morici pulled his gun and shoved it against Elijah's forehead. "One more word."

No response

"Say it!"

Elijah was scared but he spoke firmly, "I see the bitch in you."

Morici pushed his weapon so hard at Elijah that he knocked him over but didn't fire.

As Morici strutted away muttering, "I'll shoot alla you," Elijah sighed in deep relief. It had been a huge gamble, but one where he knew the likely outcome, and he'd succeeded. A man about three times his age now looked even weaker to his other five men. A middle school kid had sassed him. That could be to the captives' advantage.

Elijah suspected, as if he were an ancient witness, that since he and the others were still alive, it was because the person in charge now told Morici to keep them breathing for the time being. He also had a hunch why.

He was right. Noto didn't know how to get a message to Maya, but she was exactly why the group sat unharmed.

"Tell me more about Maya. Where else might she be?" he asked.

Raven whispered into her phone. Her boss Jason Polidore was on the other side of closed doors. "I don't know. That house in the 7th ward was where she stayed before it burned down."

Noto fumed, "You call me if you hear anything."

"I will."

"Raven, come in here!" rang out.

She rose slowly.

"Don't bother sitting down," Polidore said when she walked up to his desk.

"Okay."

"You've worked here long enough to learn a few things."

Her face was blank, wondering where he was going with this. Did he know? A bold fear rose in her.

"Am I wrong?"

"Umm, no. I mean, yes, I've learned from you. Thank you for that."

"Yeah. Do you realize, that though accessory to murder after the fact is light sentencing, something like $500 or five years, if it's before the fact, that's different."

"Why are you...?"

"Raven, do you know what a principal is?"

"Like, school?"

"In this state, a principal is anyone involved in a crime being committed. Doesn't matter if they're at the scene or not. As it stands right now, you better hope you're only a principal to kidnapping, because so help me, if any of those six get harmed."

"I don't know what you're talking about," she tried.

"Yes, you do. Better hope nothing happens to any of

them. Otherwise, you're a principal to murder times six. You gave out the address. Thought they were using it to get Maya, because you're petty like that."

"Jason. Sir. Why don't..."

"Stop. Don't insult us both by telling tales."

Polidore knew that since it couldn't yet be proven that the six had been taken at gunpoint from the house in the woods, Raven wasn't officially an accessory before the fact. So he was bluffing a bit. He considered letting her stay, not telling her what he knew, and hoping she'd end up being useful, but his multitude of sensitive files and the type of exposure that could end his career had him only waiting to see if any of her new friends called. He'd been listening via a bug under her desk when Noto called her phone just earlier.

"I'm going to walk to the front. You'll get your purse and hand over your keys. The office monitoring software on your computer at home will be immediately disabled. As of now, you are no longer working here. This is an at will employment state. Don't think of filing for unemployment or I will make your life hell. Is all this clear?"

"You don't have to..."

"Am I clear?!"

"Yes."

He looked at her with contempt. "Alright," as he got up and shoved his chair. "Time for your shady self to get the hell out."

Raven walked heavy steps. She never liked Maya, but now she was on the hook for whatever the Mafia did to six other people too. Once she got off the elevator, she called

Noto before she even made it to Poydras.

"You got me all fucked up. They're gonna put those bodies on me too. Let 'em go. Leave Maya alone. I'm serious," before she hung up.

Nick Noto sat his phone down and rubbed what remained of the hair on his head. At this rate, he'd be a cue ball by Christmas. He couldn't wait to hand over the boss seat and fall back to advising again.

Meanwhile, Maya and Zachary had returned to the house in the woods. It was still standing with no damage other than to the front door. This had allowed a few birds and squirrels to forage inside, though they hurried out once the humans returned.

"Military level. They got in. Got out," said Zachary.

"I wonder...," Maya spoke as she moved to the desk in the back. Right on top was the notebook with a pen same as her scribe Elijah had left it.

Zachary followed her. "I've been meaning to ask you. What's that all about?"

"It's partly a story. Real life story anyway. And observations, thoughts, things like that. Years down the line, I want to write my own book like *The Last Shadow*. If I make it that long."

"You will." He wanted to believe this anyway.

"My idea is to distill every page down to one essential sentence."

Zachary was stunned. "Who thinks to do something like that but you?"

"Stop," she said, thinking it was mere flattery.

"I'm serious. What would the title be?"

"Dunno if it needs one."

"Got to have a title. *The Last Shadow. Tao Te Ching. Dokkodo. Book of Five Rings.* Titles matter," he said, ready to list more.

"Okay, you're right. Remember that old movie we watched? *Rebel Without A Cause*? How about *Rebel With A Cause*?"

"Maybe. Seems kinda long."

"Am I a rebel, though?" she wondered.

"Are you a rebel? Maya, you serious? Yes, you're a rebel with a deep soul."

"Hmm, *Soul Rebel* or *Rebel Soul.*"

"Definitely," Zachary agreed.

"You get where I'm coming from? With the vendetta? It's not some filthy ideology."

He admitted, "I feel you."

"For now, though..." she pushed.

"Right, right. I'll go do recon at the warehouse. It's past Lapalco. Near the big casino. Not quite as far as the Barataria Nature Preserve."

Maya nodded. "He said way down on the West Bank."

"That fits the bill. Officially it's a fruit and vegetable warehouse, but there are state troopers sitting out there from time to time. Probably for protection. Or as security for a drug run."

"Not for mangoes."

"Nah, gotta be a Rizzo drug warehouse."

"Makes sense. All right, go see what you see. Be back before dark? It'll be a cold night."

He was concerned. "I'm fixing the door first. You're sleeping here, inside, right?"

"I have to. We'll get some heat going."

"Oh, yeah?" His voice changed a bit as he tried.

"None of that until I finish the list."

"I know, baby. One more to go."

"Zach, you're sure where he's at? That's a long drive tomorrow. I want to start early in case it snows."

He mused, "If there's any white boy super power I have, it's blending in most situations. Been there. Saw him. We're going way down in Plaquemines Parish."

"Alright," she said. "Recon only at the warehouse unless you see something going bad to deal with. I'm certain they won't harm anyone. They want me. After tomorrow, they'll get their wish. But not the way they think."

"Maya..."

She shuddered. It was already getting chilly. She didn't need to know a rare Winter Storm Warning had been announced. The air felt different. Even the animals hoped for refuge inside.

14 War At The Door

"Look at this," said Vinh Nguyen, sick and tired of hearing nothing but the sound of his own voice.

It was barely after 7:00 AM, and there was already a dusting of snow outside. By an hour later, it had begun to accumulate with what would end up becoming a little less than an inch an hour up until 5:00 PM.

"Haven't seen this since New York," he thought, remembering his days as a young man before fleeing to New Orleans in July 1991. He guessed that the others living in the long ribbon of the parish down to the Gulf, whether born and raised, or from Vietnam like him, had never experienced this. Nguyen preferred the former. The others, Vietnamese who worked in the fishing industry, had a different radar. They could tell his tale of a quiet retirement life was shaky. He could see it in their eyes. Same for the Filipino's who didn't trust him either.

They would never say anything to the authorities who wouldn't trust their hunches anyway. He could tell they knew his cloak of geniality was a cover for menace. That he was likely on the run from something or someone.

"No fishing today," he muttered, looking at his pole and tackle box. He preferred fish hooks that circled to make an ornate letter "J." He never admitted to anyone that it reminded him of how his high school crush would write the beginning of her name, "Jessica." She was angelic in his mind.

None of his crushes ever became a reality. He was

an awkward kid. As an adult, Nguyen was married to his work, and frankly, he was accustomed to a steady supply of low women. If they weren't up for it, then he had a habit of taking what he wanted. All of this corrupted his soul beyond a healthy relationship being a possibility.

"We're born alone. We die alone," he'd often said as a mantra over the past three years, but he knew better. It was bravado. He would take back any of his actions to have his sister Minh returned to the world. Her death was his fault. Would gladly sacrifice his own life to halt the painful endless memory.

North of him, all the school days had been canceled. Almost no one was going to work or defying orders and driving. One vehicle was moving through the snow, though, at a slow enough clip to add 45 minutes onto the 1-hour 15-minute drive.

As had happened over the past week, Zachary was driving Maya to handle her vendetta. 1972 Buick Gran Sport. Black. Vinyl top. Chrome everywhere. She had insisted he wait in the car no matter what, and he'd complied. He was her person. She was his. He hoped with every fiber in his soul that she'd make it through this unharmed.

They both remembered when randomly meeting at the annual Thai food fest held at the temple. He was standing at the display table admiring the variety of colorful krathong when Maya, Elijah, and Lil Bit walked up. He heard the younger two describe the beautiful handmade krathong made with a slice of banana tree trunk, folded leaves, incense sticks, and a candle. The lady on the other side of the table explained how you would launch your krathong into the water with candle and incense lit.

Maya and Zachary asked the same question at the same time, "Do you make a wish?" And that's how they both became aware of each other. Long lost friends met at last.

They ended up talking that day about everything as they would go on to do every day. Maya waited five weeks to tell him about the house in the woods, using caution in case he was somehow Rizzo-family connected or otherwise not a good fit for her.

None of their differences—he was a white man originally from Grand Rapids, Michigan who was seven years older than her—mattered. For all the things of value, they were kindred spirits.

Moving from the 9th ward of New Orleans to a house in the woods at the southern end of the parish fit right in with Zachary's mindset as a hopeful writer-to-be who studied martial arts and Eastern philosophy. He respected Maya and loved her dearly. She felt the same toward him and trusted him fully.

Arctic winds may have dropped the temperature to a rare 20° and were in the process of bringing a bizarre blizzard through the subtropical region, but Maya had one name left on her list. This one felt the most personal to her.

"I wonder what my life would be like if he'd never seen me take down those guys at the gas station," said Maya.

"Baby, you can't think that way. Gotta keep in the right here right now."

"I know," she said. "But if I'd never met him, then I'd

never have been blackmailed to fight, and everything else. There's so much that wouldn't have happened."

Zachary kept his eyes on the road. Good thing was that the snowfall wasn't quite as extreme the further south they traveled on Hwy. 23. Classic car still groaning in protest, though. They weren't heading to the end of the road, Venice, one of the southernmost points of the boot, but they wouldn't end up too far from it.

Shortly after, Zachary announced, "We're here. Passed hundreds of little white houses along the way, but this one is Vinh Nguyen's hideout. It's raised. Twelve steps up. One car parked underneath."

"Any blind spots?" Maya asked, meaning a side of the house with no windows.

"Not that I can see. Looks like he gets a view of anyone. Definitely see you once you're on the porch but not until the top of the stairs. I'm parked two doors down, by the way."

"How's it raised?"

"Wooden beams into a cement slab. There's an a/c unit toward the back."

"How much snow on the ground?"

"I'd say a couple inches. How you getting in?"

"You said no blind spots, but I know he doesn't have a window on the floor. Drive past his place, make a U-turn after a bit, then go slow and drop me off at his house."

Nguyen was a city person who'd taken to fishing. He didn't realize he missed it due to the snow day until he gravitated to his pole, took it down from its hook, and pantomimed casting it.

"Can't believe I miss sitting in Adam's Bay for hours."

He unlatched the tackle box. His live bait, aka shrimp, was in the refrigerator. Nguyen also had a few plastic shrimp with a rattle since redfish hunt by their senses instead of their eyes. That similarity to Maya wasn't lost on him.

All of a sudden, a thud resonated across the hardwood floor. Its original point of impact was from the opposite corner of the house with windows that looked out onto trees and eventually water.

Again, five seconds later, boom! And a third time.

"What the hell?" He stomped over to look outside. Nothing. Just as quickly as it started, it stopped.

Thump! It continued, steady as before in five second increments. Nguyen was angry and confused, but then it stopped again. He looked out the windows on that side of the house once more. Still nothing. Something was under the house.

He had barely started rushing across the room toward the front door to find out what was going on below when the glass in the door shattered. While in the car, Maya had unscrewed her chain whip from her bo staff so she was ready to go. She'd jumped on top of the a/c unit, swinging her weapon under the house such that the lead weight was striking the underside of the floor. Once she felt he was sufficiently distracted, she raced to the front side of the house, scaled the snowy stairs down low on all fours, and whipped the weight into the main door while running forward.

Maya was a sight. Snow covered assassin. She knew that he had surely gotten word of her blindness, so it was necessary to make an entrance. She also knew he wanted to be the big dog in any situation. Hard for an alpha to shut up.

"You fucking bitch!" he yelled as the chilly outside air began to immediately overtake the inside heat.

Maya took a running start in his direction, gauging distance from his voice. After spanning the gap while winding up the chain whip, she shot it out. He ducked and the lead weight slammed into the wall near him, putting a hole in it. Nguyen grabbed his fishing pole and a plastic shrimp bait before throwing the tackle box at her.

Pliers, net, different gauge lines, and other plastic shrimp flew or floated. One of the plastic shrimp fish hooks ended up in a house plant. The red metal box crashed short of her but skipped across the floor and struck Maya's right shin.

"Ahhhh!" she called out in pain while stopped in her tracks.

This solicited teeth from Nguyen who smiled broadly as he mocked her, "You didn't see it coming? I know your father didn't either."

Maya was furious but tried to keep from emotions. No anger. That's not how she would win. She also realized which way to shift based on the direction of his voice, and slowly stepped toward him, winding up the chain whip.

"Unnnh!" She was struck again. It did little more than sting, though. This time he had cast his line and hit her with the plastic shrimp. The rattler gave her sense it was coming, but she had no depth perception of when or at what angle it would hit her.

Nguyen knew he wouldn't take her out with the little plastic bait, knew that the hook couldn't blind her, but he also knew he wanted her at a distance. Once more, he cast his line strong at her. This time she brushed it off with her left forearm, while firing the chain whip right back, but it hit nothing.

She edged forward, bumped into the couch, and caught herself.

He snickered, "Do you remember when I told you I'm a fish and you're a bird? When we formally met in my office? You will realize I'm a fish in his element, but you, Maya, are a blind bird. One who flies into trees. Has no sense that she should sit still in a nest. You're your own worst enemy."

"You think so?" Egging him on.

"I do. I think you masquerade as a good person, but you are *máu lồn*. A shitty person."

"That's funny. I think you're a coward who ran and hid. I'm in your house in the middle of nowhere. You're a fish? Maybe a minnow. Or a shrimp who can't make it upstream. Birds swoop from the sky into the water and eat fish. Birds walk on land. I guess that means I can deal with any environment, but you can't."

"Lies!"

"You're a fish. Flopping on land. Falling from the air."

She was playing with him to bring out his emotions so he'd make a mistake.

Maya whipped the lead weight toward him and missed but took out a lamp.

Nguyen waited until the chain whip began to swing back to her before he rushed forward and shoved the glass coffee table as hard as he could. It was only a couple feet from Maya, so it slid straight into her knees and shins to knock her on her back.

Nguyen roared as he followed after the coffee table, continued with two steps to bound on top of it, and then jumped onto Maya.

He'd grabbed a tea kettle and a blender from the kitchen and gripped them tightly as he swung both against her. She took multiple blows to the head, arms, hands, while keeping in full defensive mode.

Maya expected him to tire, but she couldn't take a chance on a knockout blow from the tea kettle. Nguyen's timing was strikes on the 1 and 3-counts, like a metronome, usual for most.

After he got into his rhythm, she made sure on the 1-count that her fists were pressed against each other as her arms were extended to block blows to the head. On the 2-count, she popped out her arms, sending hammer fists upward and straight down the middle to connect with Nguyen's forehead.

"Fuck!" he called out as she reached out, grabbed teapot and blender, and threw them across the room.

Maya rose to her feet in fighting stance before Nguyen did the same.

"I trained in vovinam for decades," he spat.

"I'm ready."

After that, they spoke no more. Their fight became conjoined violence.

Vovinam, or Viet Vo Dao, was the premiere Vietnamese martial arts style. It was founded in Hanoi almost 90 years ago. Taught in New Orleans. Maya had learned the basics from Lil Bit who had watched various classes as a young child.

She knew that knees and elbows were used like Muay Thai, throws were done in Judo-style, and both high and low kicks were means to attack. At his age, Nguyen would likely be kicking low.

As expected, he started by kicking sharply to her already sore shins and swinging his leg behind to her hamstrings. Maya didn't see those coming, of course, but she could sense and block hand strikes much better. Still, he got in a few good shots.

She stopped Nguyen's right strike with her right hand, quickly delivering a left punch under his arm to an exposed rib cage.

He was better than she expected, though. If she'd been sighted, the blood streaming down her forehead would have clouded her vision, but instead it only stung.

Maya's skills were beyond Nguyen's and she was less than half his age, after all, but he had the advantage of sight, unless...

She feinted a kick before rushing in and firing rapid blows to each eye socket and the high part of his cheekbones. Her goal was to not break anything, only cause bruises, bring about swelling, and put the two of them closer to an even playing field.

He was tiring, so that helped Maya's machine gunning the attack to his face. When she pulled back to catch her breath, she could smell something in the air. It was fear, his for the first time. Before this moment, he had the arrogance that he would win by any means necessary, because that's how it had always been. When knocked down by life, he always got back up.

Maya knew how to use a certain vovinam style, but she needed a running start. This meant he'd need to be stunned into submission until she reached him. Rather than rapid fire, she began to swing for heavy impact at his belly. He tried to strike back but barely seemed to defend much less go on offense. Meanwhile, the swelling and bleeding around his eyes was building up and limiting his sight as she'd anticipated.

After prepping him with a few of these, Maya backpedaled quickly by four long steps, then ran forward, right back to where she'd been, and launched herself into the air with legs leading the way. It was a risky move, but she went for it. The last thing Vinh Nguyen saw and felt in his days upon the earth was Maya coming at him through his squinting eyes.

He saw her jump up, felt her legs tightly wrapped around his neck, and the intense pain of his life snuffed out as she delivered a flying scissors takedown. While she fell to the ground, pulling him with her, she used her legs to spin his body to the ground, and broke his neck along the way. His last radiating thought was walking with his sister Minh in the New York City park before she was shot and killed.

Maya got up and immediately returned to fighting stance, breathing heavily before realizing he wasn't getting back up. She kneeled down, checked both his breath and heart rate, took a deep breath, and left her last batch of Spanish moss.

"Everything must change, nothing stays the same," she sung as she sunk to low horse stance, reflected on Nguyen's death, before she rose and walked away.

15 Time To Say Goodbye

"It's done," Maya said when she got back into the car.

Zachary grimaced, "Ohh, Maya. Your face."

"I'm fine. We need to get the others free."

"Just a sec," he said before stepping out of the car, reaching down to scoop up snow with both hands, and compacting it like miniature snowballs.

"Here. Put this against your bruises. How do you intend to get the others free?" he asked while taking off and gauging how the increased snowfall was impacting his driving.

"You seem comfortable maneuvering in snow. Can you drive something bigger?"

He wondered where she was heading with this, but six of their group were held captive.

"You mean like a van?"

"Something like that," she responded.

"Remember, I'm from the Midwest. Used to this. But we'll want to be done before evening."

"Why's that?"

"All this'll freeze. Black ice. Treacherous to get around."

Maya heard something for the first time.

"It's actually called black ice?"

He laughed. "Yes. How about that? Your name means two things."

It was hours later, around 4:00 PM, when the main door of a certain West Bank warehouse opened. Foot was first to raise up, gun extended in front of him. Nofio Morici, his five men, and the six prisoners were stunned to see Nick Noto enter along with NYPD chief Gretchen Winters in full uniform.

"Lower your weapons!" snapped Noto. Elijah, Ayana, Cookie, Felipe, Nevaeh, and Lil Bit all looked at each other. Were they about to be freed?

"What's going on, Nick?" said Morici with a weary tone.

"Calm down." He spoke softer to Chief Winters, "That's the group of perps. The anarchists causing all the mayhem. The killing spree, arson, you name it. Their leader is a woman named Maya Gaines."

"Nick. Omerta," Morici was stunned. The interim Mafia boss was there breaking the code of silence with the head of the New Orleans police department.

Noto raised a finger to silence him while Chief Winters took out her phone. The group of captives was also feeling very confused by all this.

"Mayor Elloie, I'm here across the river. Made it through the snow. As you requested. I'm in a warehouse looking at the people—most of 'em—who killed Anthony Rizzo, his brother, and several others. Plus a multi-parish week of craziness. Burning down a new construction home. All kinds of stuff."

The chief waited and listened before responding.

"Yes, ma'am. Understood. We don't want any of the group going to trial. Their leader's out there. On the run. We'll get her. Until then, none of the group will leave here on their feet."

Chief Winters hung up, looked at Noto, and nodded.

He knew what came next.

"Nofio, handle it," he said simply, raising a finger to mean, "Wait until the chief and I leave." He'd seen no more benefit in using the prisoners as leverage to bring in Maya. At this point, it was war and that meant casualties for casualties.

With those orders, Capo Nofio Morici and his five soldiers all raised their guns to prepare for what they'd been waiting to do the past few days in a barely-heated warehouse. The fear of death became imminently terrifying to the six on the floor.

Before Nick Noto and Chief Winters got halfway to the door, it sprung open, along with the back door that led to the dock. No one was prepared for Maya to burst in the front, followed by 20 people, and Zachary to surprise with 20 more from the back. The bitter setting immediately became a sparkling dawn.

All but Maya were masked and armed with various semi-automatic assault weapons. All but Maya and Zachary were between 10-18 years old. The front and back groups moved toward each other, making a sandwich of all those already in the warehouse

"How dare you? Do you know who I am?" said an indignant Chief Winters.

Elijah and the others slowly began to slide away from Morici and his men, who along with Noto and Chief Winters were outnumbered 4-to-1 by weapons. Those pointing them were clearly tall enough to appear to be children. Kids who might have erratic trigger fingers.

"Heard you're looking for me," asked Maya. "How dare you? And everyone else. For decades, corrupt politicians and the Mafia have been stealing money meant for families. Food for kids. Job training. But you have the nerve to say, 'How dare you?'"

While Maya spoke, Zachary held up fingers for ten of those with Maya to join his group, which next moved to shield the six captives on the floor before clearly and silently forcing Morici and his soldiers to hand over their weapons. Two of the kids with Maya did the same with Chief Winters.

Maya continued, 'We can't undo the system. It's a web that's been in place for too long. So long in New Orleans that it's called 'just business.' Problem is 'just business' is shortsighted. But you don't care. Long as you get yours. Even if these kids go hungry. We can't change the world, but this is a day of reckoning."

At that, Noto, Chief Winters, Morici, and his men expected to be shot down where they stood. In actuality, there were more than a few holding weapons who were itchy to do it.

"Let's handle this in a peaceful way," said the chief.

"She's right. There's no need for...making this worse," added Noto.

As if she hadn't heard them, "Strip," said Maya.

"The fuck you talkin' about?" yelled Morici.

"You heard me. Strip. Down to underwear. Kick your clothes in front of you. Now!"

The eight who were surrounded reluctantly did as told, while the chief repeatedly told Maya she would be dealt with. Once there was a pile on the floor, Maya called out, "My people, want to do the honors?" Elijah and the other five walked over to pick up the shirts and pants now strewn about.

"We set? Let's go," said Maya to the big group of 48.

"Tell the mayor, Merry Christmas," Maya left with.

After they got outside, all the clothes were thrown into the snow before the group boarded a borrowed former school bus to return home. No chance that those inside would be following them. The 40 kids had come from Promise Home or around New Orleans once word got out. As for the assault weapons, in New Orleans they could be easily found, stolen, or bought. In this case, though, they'd been donated by a person who wanted to prove a point. As long as he got them all back. Or rather his cousin did.

Attorney Jason Polidore had business to handle against corrupt Judge Leon Mancuso. Polidore's reputation was impeccable, and he was an honorable man, but most everyone in New Orleans had someone only a call away to handle the down and dirty. Polidore's cousin fit the bill.

It was close to 5:00 PM when the slow but steadily moving school bus crossed the snow-caked Mississippi River as the sun was setting. A car skidded in front of them, but there was no collision.

Zachary knew they had limited time before the temperature would drop to below freezing and the snow, which had fallen at an inch an hour in some parts of town, would become a sheet of ice.

The repurposed party bus full of kids with guns at their feet was a felony on wheels, at least for Maya, Ayana, and Zachary, but law enforcement had other priorities. The lone blizzard in New Orleans history. The first stop was to unload the guns by Polidore's cousin Darrell's place two doors from Peace and Music. He got a little lagniappe of extra guns, courtesy of the Mafia, though no one noticed there were five extra, not six of them. Light by one.

Next, priority was to get the 40 kids home safely. It helped that 32 of them stayed at Promise Home, and by the time they pulled up there, the 7th, 8th, and 9th ward stops had happened. That only left the last three for Central City.

The roads were beginning to get slick, and Zachary was testing and feeling the brakes not fully engaging without slipping when they crossed Claiborne and pulled up to a loading dock inside an open fence at a Derbigny and Erato corner warehouse.

"Alright, all," Maya said to the remaining core group of seven. "This is our safe house for tonight. May end up being a few days."

"Maya, what about our house in the woods?" asked the youngest one, with a bright but uneven tone.

"Lil Bit, we can't go back there anymore. I'm sorry."

"I'm glad you're okay, but I'm gonna miss it."

"We all will. Since you mentioned it, those suitcases in the back aren't weapons. Your clothes are there. Everyone's. As much as we could fit."

They all trudged through what would cap at 10-inches of snow and went inside. There were more than enough couches and blankets, which was better than they'd expected.

By morning, a week before Christmas, Judge Mancuso had publicly released a statement to the press accusing Jason Polidore of aiding and abetting a murderer on the loose in an active NYPD investigation. Privately, in addition to the $50,000 drop-out-of-the-race "incentive," he had NOPD at Polidore's home to harass him, and threatening calls were made to Polidore's family by a man who sounded a lot like Foot, Nofio Morici's soldier, with extra coughing and sneezing.

"We're all back together, but it's different," Elijah said to Maya.

"That was a time I'll never forget," she said. "But remember, it was all prep for what's happening right now."

Elijah kept to himself about his vision of Maya laying on her back with snow around her. It concerned him greatly, though, so he stayed as close to her as he could.

The day after the blizzard, Maya had them doing their usual martial arts workout together, meditating in the tonglen way, and sitting in a circle together to talk.

She knew they couldn't all continue together. There would be a big hunt for her. Dividing up was the best bet at protecting them. But Lil Bit was 12-years-old and four of the others weren't much older. She couldn't leave them to the wolves of New Orleans' street life or potentially juvie jail. Couldn't live with herself for doing that.

What she could do is what she would do is what she had planned for in case their location in the woods was compromised. Ayana knew too. She was ready for it.

"Felipe, Cookie, Nevaeh, and Lil Bit, you'll go with Ayana. She's got you."

"Where we going?" wondered Cookie.

Ayana replied, "My family has a country house up in Pearl River. North of Slidell. I can commute to work from there. Plenty of room for the five of us."

Lil Bit said what the other three were thinking. "You want us?"

"Better believe it."

They didn't know what Ayana and Maya knew—she'd spent her life missing her twin brother who'd died at age 10 from the rare Batten disease. Time with the group at the house in the woods filled her up like she'd not felt since, and she'd insisted to Maya that she be in charge of the four.

"I'll miss you all so much," added Maya. "Elijah and Zachary will be going with me."

Elijah looked at her with a face showing he was fully unprepared for this but glad it was happening.

"Driver's licenses and passports with new names," said Zachary, tapping a pocket of his cargo pants.

While New Orleanians made snowmen, shot videos, sprawled out to flail snow angels, or otherwise frolicked in the winter wonderland, Police Chief Gretchen Winters was fuming and sniffling.

"I can't believe you put me in that position," she said on the phone with a methodically labored voice.

"Chief Winters," began Nick Noto. "You're new here, so let me be very clear. When your term is up. When Rosalind Elloie is no longer mayor. When hell freezes over. The Rizzo family will still be running New Orleans, Jefferson Parish, St. Bernard, St. Tammany, and the rest of Louisiana too."

"There aren't any Rizzo's left, are there? From what I hear, this means the end of organized...things being done a certain way in town. Now only living off of real estate."

Noto laughed. "Listen to me. That's what people will

think, same as they did when the Feds bugged Frank's Place and busted a bunch of guys in the 90s. File it under 'ain't dere no more.' So they say. The greatest thing Anthony Rizzo did the past 35 years was to make people think our business didn't exist anymore. Long as there's a port, long as there's people who want to party, long as there's a way to make money, it's not going anywhere. This is where it all started in the US. Not New York. Right here. New Orleans. Respectfully, fall your ass in line. I brought you to the warehouse as a goodwill gesture. How was I to know 50 kids with machine guns would show up?"

By the next day and a growing citywide hunt for Maya, more of the snow had steadily melted. Ayana's older brother came by to pick her up, along with the four kids, after he discreetly retrieved her car from the Buddhist temple parking lot, where she routinely parked it.

All eight hugged tightly and said goodbyes. That left Maya, Elijah, and Zachary.

Nick Noto didn't trust NOPD for investigative work. He knew most crimes were solved by a C.I. talking or a criminal's mistake. For that reason, he had Frankie Calamari hitting the streets. Calamari had his own informants. One of them, an intense snitch known as Domino, told him, "I seen some people going in a warehouse by the old Calliope. Might be the ones you're looking for."

It could be a long shot, Domino just hoping for cash to pay for his booze that night while he joced with friends on the Claiborne neutral ground. Calamari was feeling the pressure from Noto, though, so he made his way over from Harahan.

"You bring the book?" asked Elijah while he went through his own suitcase in the warehouse.

"Of course. There are still blank pages for you to write," said Maya.

"I'm your scribe."

"Yes, you are. And so much more."

Sariah, an ex of Zachary's, was to drive his car over from Franklin by the Almonaster split, exchange it back for her party bus, then the three would take off. Everything was moving slower than expected due to the snow, plus Sariah always took her sweet time. Not due to living on 'New Orleans time' per se, but because, in true city fashion, she juggled three jobs, a baby, family obligations, and baby daddy foolishness, so she would get there when she got there.

Calamari would've been to the warehouse sooner if not for the roads. He would've arrived before Sariah, surprised Maya, and might've gotten a clean open shot at her. That's what Noto wanted. "Take care of her," was what he ordered. He would've fired three more shots, one each at Zachary and Elijah, when they charged him. Calamari would've been efficient, the way he was trained in the military, which meant no witnesses, so no Sariah left standing either. He would've taken out his phone for photos to prove it to Noto. Would've checked their pockets for cash or anything else of value. Would've left as quickly as he came. Would've driven over to Joe's Po Boys two and a half blocks away and broken off five $20s from his roll for Domino. Would've gone over by

Beachcorner for his own drinking if Jude had the place open.

If he had come later, not sooner, Calamari would've busted into the warehouse to find no traces of Maya, Elijah, Zachary, Ayana, Felipe, Cookie, Nevaeh, or Lil Bit. Only a chain whip curled up on top of a little pile of Spanish Moss.

Instead, he pulled up as Maya and the other two were walking up to the car. Sariah and her party bus were gone.

As Calamari rushed toward them, gun drawn, Zachary immediately said, "Elijah, drive Maya out of here."

"I don't know how."

"Figure it out!" as Zachary pulled out a gun and moved toward the other man.

Maya yelled, "No! Zach!" but Elijah pulled her to the Gran Sport and had her lay down in the back seat.

Though he had very little experience driving, and, of course, no experience with snow, Elijah followed orders. He drove Maya away while watching in the rearview mirror as Zachary and Calamari went at it behind them.

"Where'd he get the gun?" they both asked in unison, seeing Zachary with a pistol, and realizing it must've come from the Mafia soldiers in the warehouse. Maya and Elijah heard a gunshot, both called out in horror, but Elijah was completing the turn on Clio, so he wasn't able to see who was hit. Didn't know if Zachary went down or if it was the other man. Maya jumped up in the back seat, called for him to turn around, and tried to reach forward and grab the wheel, but he held it firmly. She even tried to jump out of the car, but Zachary had added power locks and Elijah hit them repeatedly to keep her inside while they drove off.

Maya gave up and laid back down on the seat while she wept. Elijah looked around at the snow all around them and realized this was his prophetic vision of Maya prone on her back with snow around her. He hadn't foreseen her death. It was her escape.

Once Elijah was distracted, Maya used this to swing the back door open and roll out into the snow. She began making her way back to the intersection while Elijah slammed on the breaks.

"Maya, no."

"I can't leave him like that."

Elijah tried to pull at her, but her strength and determination had him sliding along with her. When they got to the corner, Elijah peered down the block, not knowing what he would see.

"Elijah?" asked Maya, hearing him begin to breath heavier. "What is it?"

"He's alive. Zach's alive," said Elijah, gaining energy and yelling, "Hey!" to the bent-over figure with his hands on his knees. The other man was sprawled in the street, making crimson snow.

Zachary stood upright and in disbelief.

"C'mon, let's go!" called out Elijah while Maya repeated, "Zach! Zach!"

It didn't matter that Zachary was still out of breath and reeling from what had happened. He ran through snow that had drifted up almost to his knees as if it were no real obstacle, for here was where their life in a leveetown called New Orleans ended and the rest of the world began. Soon enough they would reach their destination.

www.ingramcontent.com/pod-product-compliance
Lightning Source LLC
Chambersburg PA
CBHW062147150726
47991CB00006B/2199